KV-037-051

Trail Scum

Clay Belmont, a Texas Ranger, was sent into Peso County to clean up on the rustling, and soon found himself in far more trouble than he bargained for. Despite saving pretty Tilda Camford from being kidnapped, he managed to get himself captured by some hard cases who threatened to bury him in the desert.

But help was at hand in the form of Baldy Jex, an ex-Ranger who knew how to handle a gun. Together their investigations led them to badmen who spoke of Orton as the boss, but Kane Orton, owner of the big KO ranch, denied rustling, despite some of his crew being involved.

The crooked business developed quickly into shooting, and it was not until the gun smoke was clearing that the answers to the questions bothering Belmont became plain to see.

By the same author

Range Grab
Bank Raid
Range Wolves
Gun Talk
Violent Trail
Lone Hand

Trail Scum

CORBA SUNMAN

A Black Horse Western

ROBERT HALE · LONDON

© Corba Sunman 2001
First published in Great Britain 2001

ISBN 0 7090 6829 8

Robert Hale Limited
Clerkenwell House
Clerkenwell Green
London EC1R 0HT

The right of Corba Sunman to be identified as
author of this work has been asserted by him
in accordance with the Copyright, Designs and
Patents Act 1988.

DERBYNIWYD/ RECEIVED	1 1 NOV 2008
CONWY	
GWYNEDD	
MÔN	
COD POST/POST CODE	LL5 1AS

Typeset by
Derek Doyle & Associates, Liverpool.
Printed and bound in Great Britain by
Antony Rowe Limited, Wiltshire.

One

He was crossing the desert at a steady lope, tall and lean, a big man riding a chestnut stallion that had carried him tirelessly since daybreak across the torturous stretch of sand covering that part of the south-west line between Mexico and Texas. His faded, travel-stained black Stetson was pulled low over keen blue eyes that were determined in their search of his arid surroundings, particularly the ground stretching out interminably before him. He was following hoofprints, which were the only link between him and the badman he sought.

A fine mantle of clinging grey dust covered his raw-boned figure, lying thickly in the folds of his wash-faded blue shirt and the black neckerchief tied at the nape of his neck and lying in loose folds across his throat. He wore Texas leg chaps, and looked like a man who had urgent business in the Texas town of Broken Ridge, only a few miles now to the north. From time to time, his bronzed right hand dropped to the flared butt of the .45 pistol riding in the dark, scuffed, cutaway holster on his hip.

Clay Belmont instinctively watched his surroundings as he rode, occasionally glancing rearwards along his back-trail, for this was a raw, primitive, turbulent land of lawlessness, where men had ready trigger-fingers and smouldering passions. Its sparse population contained a large percentage of hard men who had little regard for law and order and no respect for their fellows, but they were countered by a small percentage of tough men who were imbued with an innate appreciation of honesty and indomitable determination to force justice into the unenlightened corners of the Lone Star State.

Belmont was one of the law bringers, a man who was ready to lay down his life for the intangible law that governed him. His blood ran deep and red like the blood of his long-dead father, who had helped build up the organization that ranged across Texas seeking out the wrong-doers, the trail scum who stole, killed as if by instinct, and owed allegiance to no one but themselves as they lived by the law of the gun.

The afternoon slouched by, timeless and brooding under the brassy sun. The chestnut plodded on patiently, the sounds of its passing muffled by the great silence of this desolate land. Only the creaking of saddle leather disturbed the peace of centuries, and both horse and rider sensed that they were cocooned in this hell of silence and heat.

To Belmont's left, seeming close but lying at least sixty miles distant behind the shimmering heat-haze, a line of mountains thrust up its mass to form the western horizon, and Belmont knew from their position exactly where he was in this featureless land. By nightfall he should be riding into Broken Ridge, Texas, ready to fight the growing lawlessness blighting Peso County, unless the tracks he followed veered away from the distant township.

His instructions from Captain McQuade of Texas

Rangers Company D had been succinct, understated. Belmont had to ride into Mexico on the trail of the wanted outlaw Morgan Piercey and bring him back dead or alive. If Piercey was killed, or not located, then Belmont should ride back into Texas and make for Broken Ridge in Peso County to deal with a problem that had arisen there. Asa Camford, owner of the Bar C ranch in Peso County, an ex-Texas Ranger who had ridden with Belmont's father in the old days, had complained of local rustling and murder, and his testimony could be accepted as gospel and acted on without question.

Belmont had failed to find Piercey in any of the outlaw's known haunts south of the border, although there were indications that he had been in the area recently and had probably learned that a Ranger was on his trail. Now, Belmont was heading for Broken Ridge, and he had spotted tracks in the sand which might have been left by his quarry so he was alert for trouble. Piercey was reputed to have the instincts of a snake and had never been bested in ten years of outlawry.

The chestnut suddenly twitched its ears, pointing them to the left, and Belmont, ever alert, read the sign instantly. He eased his left foot out of the stirrup and swung sideways to the right, leaning low in the saddle as he clawed his long-barrelled .45 from its holster. The weapon was cocked and ready in his hand as he clung to the saddlehorn and ducked to peer under the neck of his horse. He heard the flat crack of a rifle, and a bullet crackled over his saddle, cleaving through the space his heart would have occupied but for the chestnut's warning.

Belmont saw gunsmoke drifting from a large rock over to the left some fifty yards distant and vacated the saddle instantly, dropping lithely to the ground. The chestnut snorted and cantered out of the line of fire then stopped and stood with lowered head, awaiting the outcome of the disturbance.

Slithering into a hollow, Belmont removed his Stetson and raised up to observe. A second puff of gunsmoke erupted from the right of the yellowish rock and, as the crack of the rifle rang out, a slug struck the sand by his side. He caught sight of a furtive movement as his ambusher began to shift position and his gun blasted twice. Booming echoes hammered and the ambusher twisted and dropped out of sight.

Belmont got to his feet, gun ready, and stalked towards the rock, certain he had at least winged the ambusher. He gave the rock plenty of space in circling it, and paused when he saw a man stretched out on his face, a discarded rifle lying close to his inert body. There was a horse standing nearby with trailing reins.

Belmont went forward and checked the man, his lips pulling tight against his teeth when he saw two bullet wounds in the chest, instantly recognizing Piercey. The outlaw had finally reached the end of his trail. Belmont turned away and returned to his mount. He patted the chestnut's muzzle and the horse snorted.

'Thanks, ol' hoss! Yuh saved me again! I sure wish I had your instincts. It would make my job a whole lot easier.' He reached for the canteen suspended from the saddlehorn, removed his neckerchief and knocked the dust from it, then soaked the limp cloth and wiped the chestnut's soft muzzle, removing clogging dust from its flared nostrils. He shook the canteen to gauge its contents, poured a small quan-

tity of the precious liquid into his hat and offered it
to the animal. The brackish water did little more
than moisten the chestnut's tongue but it would
suffice until they reached Broken Ridge. Belmont
patted the dusty neck of the animal and swung into
his saddle to return to the dead man.

He rolled Piercey in a slicker that was tied to the
man's cantle and slung the body face down across
the saddle. When he went on he was fully alert to the
possibility of more danger riding ahead of him; but
his tiredness had receded and he was ready for trouble.

Darkness came suddenly, long shadows stabbing
down from the distant peaks. The sun lowered its
brassy face beyond the tallest mountain and velvet
darkness blotted out the arid landscape. Stars bright-
ened in the sky, and shortly a slim crescent of the
moon appeared, shedding pale light upon the final
stretch of Belmont's journey.

When he saw twinkling lights of Broken Ridge in
the distance he had just realized that the shifting
sand underfoot had given way to poor grassland,
which, he knew, would change to better vegetation
further north. The chestnut had quickened its pace,
and Belmont marvelled that the animal could raise a
canter after the seemingly endless miles of burning
wasteland it had traversed since dawn without food
or water.

It was middle evening when he reached the south-
ern fringe of Broken Ridge and reined up at the
adobe stable. A lantern was burning in the entrance
and, as he dismounted, a slight figure emerged from
the low building to greet him.

'Howdy, mister. Looks like you rode far.' The
youth reached out a hand for the chestnut's bridle.

Trail Scum

'I'll take care of my horse.' Belmont ignored the youth's comment.

'Say, is that man dead on the other horse?' the youngster suddenly demanded, the tone of his voice rising a notch or two in shock.

'Men are usually dead when they ride in that position. Where will I find the local law?'

'The sheriff's office is halfway along the street, on the left. Did you kill him, mister?'

'Yeah.'

'Are you a lawman?'

Belmont did not reply. He led both horses to a water trough, permitting them to drink sparingly and taking them away before they could gulp their fill.

'Give the chestnut another drink later, huh?' he said. 'He's had a dry day.' He tied the reins of the horse carrying the dead outlaw to a hitching rail. 'This one will be back presently.'

'Sure thing.' The youth followed as Belmont led the chestnut into the stable and put oats and chaff in a manger. Then he stood by while the chestnut was stripped of its gear. 'You want I should run along to the law office and tell Herb Grant about this dead feller?'

'Nope. I'll deliver him personal to the sheriff.' Although he had eaten nothing since breakfast, Belmont did not skimp on taking care of his horse. In his book the animal came first, and only when he was satisfied that it was comfortable would he begin to think of himself.

'Don't forget to water him again,' he reminded, handing a silver dollar to the youth. He patted the chestnut's neck. 'Take care of my gear until I come back for it, huh?'

'Sure thing!' the youth exclaimed. 'Anything you say, mister.'

Belmont left the barn and grasped the reins of the horse carrying Piercey. He had never been in Broken Ridge before, and looked around keenly as he led the horse along the gloomy street. He passed a big saloon, and paused to peer in over the batwings to see about twenty men crowding the bar. A banjo was tinkling out a Mexican tune, and for a moment Belmont hesitated. His insides were parched, his throat burning with thirst, but he resisted the temptation and went on until he came to a building over the doorway of which an illuminated board contained a two-word legend: LAW OFFICE.

Belmont wrapped the reins around a hitching rail and pushed open the door of the office. He stepped inside and found himself looking at a big, rough-looking man seated at a cluttered desk, chair tilted back on two legs and his feet resting on the desk top. He was busy scanning a mail-order catalogue, and looked up guiltily when he heard the door open. His heavy face slowly assumed a brutal scowl as he took in Belmont's appearance. Then his feet crashed to the floor and he grunted as he stood up. Although he was six feet tall, Belmont topped him by three inches.

'Who in hell are you?' A deputy sheriff star was pinned to the man's shirt front and he wore a cartridge belt strapped around his thick waist, the greased holster containing a well-polished six-gun.

Belmont took an instant dislike to the man's manner and closed the door at his back with a spurred heel. He looked the man in the eyes, his lips pulling into a thin, humourless smile.

'And who in hell are you?' he countered in a deceptively soft tone, blue eyes shining like glass in the harsh lamplight filling the office.

'Sassy, huh? You just ride in? You look like a

stranger to me.' The deputy's right hand was down by his side and Belmont, noting a slight twitch in the thick fingers, sensed eagerness in the man's brusque manner. 'I don't like strangers who ride into town after dark, mister. Start any trouble around here and you won't get throwed in the hoosegow. We bury troublemakers in Broken Ridge, and there's been a few of them this past year.'

'Is that so?' Belmont nodded slowly. 'I've got a body for you. An outlaw face down across his saddle name of Morgan Piercey. Where's the sheriff?'

'Herb Grant rode out for a few days, leavin' me in charge. You kill Piercey?'

'Yeah. I'll give you the details later. Right now I got a burning thirst and I'm empty as a drum.' Belmont turned to the door.

'Hold it, mister.' Belligerence crept into the deputy's tone. 'Who in hell are you? Do you figger you can walk in here, tell me you killed a man, then leave without explaining? We don't run that kind of law in Peso County. Cool your heels and I'll handle this.'

'What's your name?' Belmont responded.

'Roscoe Dayne. You a bounty hunter? How'd you meet up with Morg Piercey?'

'I'm Clay Belmont, Texas Ranger. You'll have had a wire from Captain McQuade informing this office I'd be riding in to operate in Peso County.'

'Texas Ranger, huh?' Dayne scratched the dark stubble on his blunt chin. 'Yeah, I got the lowdown on you. It came through yesterday. So someone in the county contacted the Rangers, huh? And then you ride in with a body you claim is Morg Piercey.' He showed strong white teeth in a mirthless grin. 'This I got to see.'

Belmont half turned, opened the door then stepped aside, and Dayne went out into the darkness, lifting a lantern off the front wall in order to take a close look at the motionless figure draped across the saddle of the waiting horse. The silence of the night seeped into the office.

Belmont looked around. There was a gun rack on the back wall containing an assortment of rifles and shotguns. A barred door, also in the back wall, led into a passage giving access to cells. On another wall there was a notice board with a number of hard faces staring fixedly out of wanted posters pinned there. One face was that of Morgan Piercey, and Belmont crossed to it and tore the poster from the board. He turned to face Dayne as the deputy came back into the office, holding out the dodger.

'Yeah. It's Piercey all right.' Dayne's voice was hoarse. 'You must have got the drop on him. Did you have to kill him?'

'He shot at me from cover.' Belmont shrugged. 'Inform my headquarters he's dead, and take care of that horse outside. I'll talk to you later.'

This time the deputy did not protest, and Belmont left the office and scuffed through the dust back along the gloomy street. He reached the hotel and entered the lobby, where an oldish woman wearing a plain black dress stood behind the reception desk. She looked up at him, instinctively smiling a welcome. In her fifties, she had a face that was deeply wrinkled. Her lank hair was grey and straggly. Belmont responded with a nod and signed the register. 'Can I get some food now?' he queried. 'I last ate at dawn this morning.'

The woman grimaced as she glanced at the big clock ticking monotonously on the back wall. 'I'll see what I can do,' she said. 'It's rather late, but it should be all right, although I can't promise a regular meal.'

'Anything will do,' Belmont replied. 'I could eat a rattler if it was fried with onions.'

'We never have snake on the menu,' she responded in kind, smiling, and about ten years seemed to fall from her features. She looked at the register and her eyes widened when she saw that he had written his occupation beside his signature. 'You're a Ranger!' she gasped. 'One has been expected for weeks.'

'Is that so, ma'am?' He shook his head slowly. 'I didn't know I was being sent here until a week ago. The town must have been expecting someone else. There's trouble hereabouts, I've been told.'

'A lot of trouble.' She pursed her lips. 'Are you the only Ranger they sent? I'd have thought a whole company would have been ordered in.'

'I can always get help should I need it.' Belmont smiled. His tone was gentle, indicating that he appreciated the trouble he was giving her. 'I'll go to my room and clean up. If you can get me some food it should be ready by the time I come down again, huh?'

She nodded and handed over a key. 'Room Eight. Up the stairs and turn to the right. Each door is numbered. I'll have a meal ready for you in about ten minutes.'

Belmont took the key and thanked her. So he had been expected. That meant any local badmen would be on the alert. He thought of Roscoe Dayne and wondered if the big deputy had passed on to the local lawless element the contents of the wire he had received from Ranger headquarters.

He went up to his room, washed and shaved, and then cleaned his gun. When he went down to the small dining-room a young girl appeared carrying a tray, and Belmont's nostrils twitched when he caught the smell of cooked food.

He ate the meal hungrily, washing it down with hot coffee. Then he was ready to look around Broken Ridge, and sauntered from the hotel to walk through the shadows along the main street. He had an innate thirst that no amount of coffee would assuage, and paused at the batwing doors of the big saloon he had passed on his way to the law office. The place was busy, and he shouldered through the batwing doors and went to the bar.

Two 'tenders were busy serving the noisy throng. Belmont waited several moments, then slapped the top of the bar. The nearest 'tender glanced at him, took a second, closer look, and stepped in front of him, smiling a welcome dredged up from the recesses of his mind.

'Whiskey and a beer chaser,' Belmont said.

The man nodded, serving him quickly. Belmont flipped a silver dollar on the bar but the 'tender shook his head.

'You're the Ranger, ain't yuh?' he demanded.

'Sure thing.' Belmont was aware of the silence that settled around him, and the men on either side eased back to give him more elbow room.

'Your first drink is on the house,' the barman said quietly. 'The boss, Deke Farley, left orders that you don't pay.'

'Is that so?' Belmont gulped the whiskey and nodded. 'And this is a drop of the better stuff, I guess.' He drank half the contents of the big glass of beer then licked his lips and set down the glass. 'You wouldn't believe how long I've been waiting to wet my whistle.'

'Come in across the desert from Mexico, didn't you?' the bartender asked.

'You got it in one. Where'd you get the news from? I ain't been in town more than half an hour.'

'Roscoe Dayne, the deputy, was in here fifteen minutes ago. Said you nailed Morg Piercey. That outlaw sure had a good run before you caught up with him. I reckon he was mixed up in the rustling they got on this range. They didn't come any tougher than Morg Piercey'

Belmont nodded and finished his drink. 'Thanks,' he said. 'I'll pay for my drinks after this. See you around.'

He departed, and stood outside the saloon with his back to the front wall, listening to the excited voices in the saloon discussing him and Piercey's death. He peered around into the shadows. A few lanterns were burning here and there, set on awning posts along the street and forming small pools of yellow glare in the dense velvet darkness. They did not aid his vision, and he walked on, making for the livery barn, wanting to collect his saddle-bags.

The lantern still burned over the doorway to the stable, and Belmont's feet made no sound as he walked through the shadows to the wide doorway. He paused at the front corner of the barn, remaining in darkness to study the wide area of yellow light illuminating the big doorway, feeling disinclined to expose himself so starkly. Then he turned to his left and walked along the side of the barn, making for the rear. He paused at the back corner of the building to give his eyes time to adjust to the deeper gloom, uneasy at the way the big entrance was lit.

There was a back entrance to the barn, which gave access to the small pole corral by which he was standing, and Belmont slipped between the poles and walked to the narrow door in the rear of the building. He checked his six-gun, easing it in his holster, and halted beside the door to apply an eye to a knothole in the back wall. Looking into the barn, he saw lantern light smearing the big front entrance. When his eyes became adjusted to the glare he spotted two men standing inside the barn, one either side of the doorway, each holding a drawn six-gun in his hand, their attention on the lighted area out front.

Belmont nodded slowly as he considered, then drew his gun and sneaked in through the back doorway to take cover in an empty stall. He eased forward, closing the distance to the main entrance, watching the two waiting men intently, certain that he had walked in upon a gun trap.

'Where in hell is Orton?' one of the men suddenly demanded, his harsh voice filled with impatience. 'I got somethin' better to do than loaf around this barn.'

'We got a job on and you've been well paid for your part in it,' the other replied. 'Shut up, will you? Do you wanta tip them off we're waiting? This better go off without any trouble or you'll be looking for another job.'

Belmont frowned. By the sound of it they were not waiting for him. He eased forward into another stall and crouched, settling himself to wait. If these two were laying for someone then he wanted to be in on it. He studied the two men while he waited, although it was too gloomy in the barn to make out much detail. He holstered his gun and listened to the muttered conversation. One man was taciturn, irritated by his companion's talk, for the other kept running off at the mouth, eternally complaining about everything that came to his mind.

After some ten minutes had passed the sound of approaching hooves out front silenced both men. Belmont tensed. He saw two riders materialize out of the gloom beyond the patch of light and his teeth clicked together when he saw that one was a young woman dressed in range clothes and wearing a flat-crowned plains hat. She sprang lightly to the ground and came forward into the barn, leading her horse. Her companion was an older man who dismounted slowly and followed her while complaining about his aches and pains.

'Do leave off, Baldy,' the girl remonstrated. 'You're not that old to be moaning about your health. Dad won't pension you off, if that's what you're angling for.'

'You know better'n that, Tilda! I ain't never gonna retire. You're stuck with me to the end of my days.'

He followed her into the barn as he spoke, and one of the waiting men stepped in close and slammed the barrel of a six-gun against his skull. The girl whirled at Baldy's yell of pain, in time to see him pitch to the ground. The second man moved towards her, gun in hand, and she froze.

'What do you want?' she demanded. 'If you've hurt Baldy you'll be neck deep in trouble.'

'We're gonna take you out for a little ride so shut your mouth and keep it closed or you'll get some of what Baldy got. He ain't hardly been touched so forget about him. Just do like you're told and you won't get bad hurt.'

Belmont drew his gun and moved forward, covering the distance to the man with a couple of long strides. He swung his Colt upwards and then crashed the barrel down against the man's forearm, aiming for the wrist. The hardcase uttered a yell of pain and his hand fell limply to his side, the gun slipping from his suddenly nerveless fingers. Belmont continued to move forward and lunged against the man with his left shoulder, at the same time thrusting the toe of his left boot behind the man's nearest heel. The hardcase reeled backwards, losing his balance as his heel struck Belmont's boot. He fell to the ground and Belmont aimed a shrewd kick at his head, which, when it connected, made the man lose all interest in the rapidly changing situation.

Belmont heard the girl's gasp of shock as he appeared at her side and he stepped around her as the second man straightened from examining Baldy. Gun levelled, Belmont waited for the man's instinctive reaction, and the hardcase didn't disappoint him, tilting the muzzle of his gun upwards in an attempt to cover Belmont.

'Drop the gun,' Belmont advised. 'I don't feel like another killing today.'

The man hesitated, his eyes narrowing as he gauged his chances. Belmont fired instantly, aiming for the right shoulder and, as his gun flamed and crashed, the six-gun flew out of the man's hand and he spun away, grasping his shattered shoulder as he dropped to one knee and hunched over.

Belmont waited for the thunder of the shot to fade, his blue eyes watching the girl's face. She was pretty, with dark hair and brown eyes, and he noticed that the crown of her hat barely reached as high as his shoulder. She was shocked rigid by the turn of events, and he smiled thinly as he stepped around her again to scoop up the gun dropped by the gunman he had knocked down.

'Lucky I was around,' he remarked. 'Tell me who

you are and why these hardcases were waiting in here to give you trouble.'

She went forward a couple of paces and peered coolly into the face of the man Belmont had rendered unconscious. When she looked at him again there was an unreadable emotion glinting in her dark eyes. She shook her head and moved around until she could see the face of the man with the bullet-busted shoulder.

'They're both strangers to me,' she said, coming back to Belmont. 'Trail scum! That's what they are, and there are too many of their kind gathering in Peso County. It's about time the law made some kind of effort to put them down.'

Her tone was scornful, and Belmont guessed what she was feeling. She went to the unconscious Baldy's side and dropped to her knees, pushing her hat from her dark hair so that it hung down her back suspended by its chinstrap across her throat. She patted the old man's cheek with no result.

'Baldy? Are you all right?' she demanded worriedly, then looked up at Belmont. 'Do you think he's badly hurt? He was hit on the head with a gun barrel.'

Belmont walked to where she was kneeling and, as he let his concentration shift to the old man on the ground, he caught a flicker of movement in the big front doorway. Dropping into a defensive crouch, he spun to face the danger, his right hand flashing to the butt of his holstered gun. A tall man was standing in the doorway, his face shadowed by the wide brim of his hat. Belmont continued his movement, dropping to one knee as he cocked his pistol, and he was prepared to fight for the newcomer was drawing a gun, and he was fast . . . .

Two

Alarm stabbed through Belmont as he flashed into action. A split-second behind the stranger's draw, he was faster, but as his gun lined up on the newcomer's chest he was disconcerted by a glint of bright metal on the man's shirt front. Was it a law badge? He hurled himself to the left and shifted his aim a fraction for a wing shot. There was no way he could stop the man from drawing, and he thumbed off a shot that filled the barn with smoke and thunderous echoes.

The bullet struck the newcomer high in the chest and sent him whirling away. His legs lost their strength and he pitched to the ground. Belmont got slowly to his feet, gun smoking in his hand, noting that the girl was frozen on her knees, her hands clasped together and pressed against her lips.

Glancing around, Belmont saw that the man he had kicked in the head was still unconscious, and the other, who had felled Baldy, was on his knees, still hunched over and pressing a hand to his shoulder. The newcomer lay in the doorway, flat on his back with both arms outstretched. Belmont went to his side and gazed at the star pinned to the man's shirt front. He shook his head. This guy was the town marshal, and had been intent on gunning him down without warning.

'That's Sim Goymer!' the girl volunteered in a high-pitched tone. She came to Belmont's side and grasped his left forearm with a trembling hand. 'He was gonna shoot you in cold blood. Have you killed him? It might be better if he is ready for planting because he's a bad man to cross. How he ever became a lawman I'll never know. He's no better than the rest of the scum crowding into this county.'

'There are some lawmen like that.' Belmont spoke softly as he reached into his left breast pocket and produced his Ranger badge, a small star of shiny metal set in a circle, which he pinned to his shirt front. He made a practice of never wearing the badge on the trail because it made too good an aiming mark for any ambusher who wanted to take a shot at him, but he needed it on show in a community to avoid accidents happening. He would give this local lawman the benefit of the doubt until he learned the facts surrounding the man's murderous attack.

The girl gazed at the badge Belmont had pinned on, her eyes wide with shock. He smiled.

'I can't tell by your expression if you're pleased or not by this,' he observed, jerking a thumb at the badge.

'To say I'm shocked is an understatement.' Her oval face was without blemish, the features small, well formed and filled with strength of character. 'My father has been waiting weeks for a Ranger to arrive in the county. He was a Texas Ranger himself in the old days, before he became too old to live that kind of a life.'

'Asa Camford!' Belmont nodded, aware of a surge

of interest for her in his breast, for he found her good to look at. Her charm was tugging intangibly at his senses. 'I was told to contact him at the Bar C ranch. I'll be riding out there first thing in the morning. Glad I was able to help you out of a nasty situation, Miss Camford. Why was that pair intent on kidnapping you?'

'To put even more pressure on my father, I expect.' She shook her head slowly. 'He warned me not to ride around without taking precautions, but I didn't believe the situation was this bad.'

'And now you've found out the hard way that it is.' Belmont nodded. 'Do you have business in town?'

'I need to talk to the sheriff so I took the risk of coming in with just Baldy for protection.'

'I heard that the sheriff is away on a trip at the moment. Will you stay the night in town? I'll be happy to escort you back to the ranch when I ride to Bar C to talk to your father.'

'I plan on staying here tonight.' She turned to look at Baldy, who was beginning to groan and stir.

Belmont dropped to one knee beside the prostrate town marshal. The man was unconscious; Belmont's bullet had struck him much lower in the chest than had been intended. He arose, and at that moment the youth who had attended him when he first arrived at the stable appeared in the doorway. Belmont's gun leaped into his hand and the youngster backed off nervously, his hands lifting in sudden fear, his wide gaze drawn to the silver badge on Belmont's shirt front.

'Is there a doctor in town?' Belmont asked.

'Doc Judd,' the youngster responded, shaking his head in disbelief at the sight of four men lying on the ground.

'Go fetch him and be quick.'

The youth nodded and darted away. Belmont heard a harsh voice out there in the darkness beyond the entrance asking a question. The next instant Roscoe Dayne, the deputy sheriff, appeared in the doorway, gun in hand, his heavy face set in a belligerent scowl. He waggled the weapon uncertainly as he took in the grim scene awaiting his narrowed eyes.

'What was that shooting?' he demanded. His gaze flicked to Belmont and he lowered his gun when he saw the badge on Belmont's shirt. 'Uhuh!' He nodded slowly. 'I shoulda guessed you'd be mixed up in whatever was going on. So what happened here?'

'I'll tell you what happened,' Tilda Camford cut in, and proceeded to explain in a scathing tone, as if she held the deputy personally responsible for what had occurred.

Dayne listened attentively, and when she lapsed into silence he nodded. 'Heck, you've been warned about riding around this county alone, Miss Camford,' he said easily. 'Like your pa told you, it's plain asking for trouble.'

'It's a fine state of affairs when a girl can't go about her lawful business without being accosted by scum like these,' she countered spiritedly. Bending over the stirring Baldy, she put a hand under his right shoulder to help him to his feet. The old man staggered when he was upright, and Belmont stepped in to support him with a powerful arm, his attention still on the deputy sheriff, uncertain yet of the lawman's intentions. His instincts had warned him at the outset that Dayne was not a good lawman.

'Did you shoot Goymer?' Dayne demanded, looking down at the town marshal, who was groaning and stirring.

Belmont went forward and kicked the marshal's discarded gun out of reach as the man's right hand instinctively scrabbled for the weapon.

'He came in drawing his gun. I had no choice but to bore him. I saw his badge at the last moment and pulled the shot some or he'd be dead now. Belmont went across to the other man he had shot, who was still on one knee and clasping his shattered shoulder. 'Take a look at this jasper. Have you any idea who he is?'

Dayne came to his side and looked down at the wounded hardcase. He grasped the man's hair and dragged his head back in order to see the rugged face.

'I've seen him around town. Him and the other one rode in mebbe a week ago, and they've done nothing but hang around the saloons, drinking and gambling. Seemed to me they was waiting for someone to show up or something to happen. Is that one over there shot as well?'

'No. He's sleeping off a kick in the head.' Subdued voices were talking out in the darkness beyond the doorway, and Belmont moved uneasily, aware that he made an easy target standing in the lamplight. 'Jail these two until I can find out what their business is. They were planning to kidnap Miss Camford. I heard 'em talking about it.'

A short, slightly built man carrying a black leather medical bag came in through the doorway, followed by the stable-boy.

'What happened here, Dayne?' Doc Judd dropped to one knee and examined the town marshal as the deputy explained what had happened.

Belmont turned to check Baldy. The old man was unsteady on his feet, and he looked at Belmont's big figure, shaking his head. Then his glazed eyes spotted the Ranger badge on Belmont's shirt front and his mouth opened and snapped shut a couple of times like a fish out of water before he managed to speak.

'You're a Ranger!' he said hoarsely, forcing a grin. 'At last! My prayers have been answered.' He paused and shook his head, then groaned. 'That's if young men today are as good as we were in my day.'

'Baldy was a Ranger along with my father,' Tilda Camford said.

'Then you must have known my father,' Belmont responded. 'He rode with Asa Camford.'

'What was his name?' Baldy demanded.

'I'm Clay Belmont. My father was known as Wild Bill.'

'The hell you say!' Baldy immediately forgot about his aching head and grasped Belmont's hand, shaking it vigorously. 'Is Wild Bill still alive? I ain't heard about him in a coon's age. He was rightly named. Wild he certainly was, and a good man when the chips were down.'

'He's been dead nearly five years.' Belmont's voice was unemotional. 'He happened to walk in on a bank hold-up Sonora way. He killed two of the robbers before the others downed him. He was always ready to fight and die for law and order.'

'He was a great man,' Baldy said harshly. 'We was good pards. And you could be a chip off the old block, the way you put this scum down in the dust. Ain't that Sim Goymer in the doorway? Glory be! You're sure gonna make a big difference around here, Clay. It'll be like the old days, else I miss my guess.'

Doc Judd came to the ex-Ranger's side. 'What

happened to you, Baldy? How'd they manage to get the better of you?'

'Just a crack on the head, Doc,' the old man responded. 'Got the drop on me. But I guess they can't hurt me by banging on my dome. They don't know I keep my brains in my feet.'

Doc Judd was pressing the oldster's skull with sensitive fingers. 'Nothing broken,' he diagnosed. 'But you look like you could be concussed. Take it easy for a couple of days, Baldy. If the headache is still with you in forty-eight hours then come in and see me.'

'Shucks, it ain't nothing, Doc. A mule kick in the head couldn't hurt me none.' Baldy staggered as he spoke and Belmont supported him with a strong hand under his right armpit. 'This here young feller is Wild Bill Belmont's boy, Doc. You've heard me and Asa talk about Wild Bill. And Clay here is a Ranger. He's following the tracks his father made. And by the looks of this shoot-out he's as good as his father ever was, and that's saying something.'

'Glad to know you.' Doc Judd smiled as he shook hands with Belmont. 'Even if you are going to give me a lot of extra work around here. But the whole county is diseased, just as if it's got gangrene, and honest folk will not be safe until the poison has been rooted out. Unfortunately the only cure for such an ailment is gunsmoke and lead. I just hope you're up to the task.'

'Thanks. I'll do my best.' Belmont ejected the spent cartridges from his pistol and thumbed fresh ones into the empty chambers from the loops on his belt. He slid the weapon back into his holster with a slick motion that was not unnoticed by those standing around him. He looked around and saw the stable-boy standing nervously in the doorway. 'I came in for my saddle-bags,' he said, and the youngster darted into the dusty office to the right of the doorway.

With his saddle-bags across his left shoulder, Belmont escorted Tilda Camford and Baldy along the street. A crowd had gathered outside the stable and Belmont felt exposed as he walked with the girl and the old man. Baldy was leaning on his arm, and Belmont was concerned about his father's old friend.

'You better get yourself bedded down somewhere, Baldy,' he suggested. 'You need to get some sleep for a few hours.'

'There ain't nothing wrong with me,' the oldster replied ferociously. 'I'm ready for some action. I was laying it on a bit thick back there at the stable. You've come into Peso County to handle the trouble here, and I can put you on the right trail. I've been watching points and I figure I got it dead to rights.'

'Baldy's been talking like this for weeks,' Tilda said sharply. 'And he knows what he's talking about so hear him out, Clay. He'll jaw your ears off if you don't pay any heed.'

'Orton is back of all the trouble round here,' Baldy said vehemently. 'I've heard his name mentioned on more than one occasion.'

'Who's Orton?' Belmont enquired. 'One of these two men mentioned that name before you arrived.'

'He bought the old Double Arrow spread to the north of Bar C about five years back.' Baldy massaged his head gingerly. 'There wasn't no trouble hereabouts before he showed up. But since he came into the county everything has changed, and for the worse. Hardcases are drifting in, and the crew Orton has hired don't look like regular cowhands. You mark my words: Orton is back of the trouble.'

'We'll talk later, Baldy,' Belmont promised. 'You rode into town to talk to the sheriff, Tilda. Is anything wrong?'

'I've seen strangers on our range, and they don't look like they're just riding through. We've been hit hard by rustlers, but although Pa has hired extra crew the losses continue. I don't think Pa will take much more. And Baldy makes it much worse. He's always talking about taking the law into his own hands, but you can bet the minute they start anything the whole range will flare up into open war and innocent people will get hurt.'

'That won't happen now I've arrived,' Belmont said firmly. 'I figure to put a bridle on the trouble around here.'

'But you're only one man,' she protested.

'One Ranger!' Baldy corrected, chuckling harshly. 'That makes a big difference, Tilda. You watch the badmen around here when Clay gets to work.'

Belmont shook his head, wishing it could be that easy, but he remained silent. He needed time in which to look around and get the feel of the business. But at the moment he was tired and needed rest before this new case swallowed him with its action and complexities.

His eyes were cold and alert beneath his hatbrim, checking the shadows around him as they went along the street towards the hotel. He was keenly aware of the girl at his side. The softness of her voice had touched him, stirred natural longings in his breast, and he sensed that his mental equilibrium had been disturbed by her presence. He made an effort to keep his concentration upon what he had to do, and was relieved when they reached the door of the hotel. He touched the brim of his hat as he prepared to withdraw from the girl's company.

'I hope you're going to stay out of trouble until morning,' he said. 'I've had a tough week and I need to sleep before I throw myself into this job.'

'Don't worry about us.' Tilda spoke cheerfully. 'If the sheriff is away then I've had this ride into town for nothing. I plan to turn in now, and Baldy won't even visit the saloon tonight, will you, Baldy?' There was a tone in her voice which promised trouble for the ex-Ranger if he did not agree.

The old man shook his head although his expression belied his agreement. 'I'm getting a mite old to waste my sleeping time,' he retorted. 'Beer don't seem to taste the same these days. It's the price we old 'uns have to pay. You make hay while you're still young enough to enjoy life, Clay.'

Belmont smiled and took his leave of them. He went up to his room, but, although he was weary he did not turn in. He sat down on the bed and cleaned his gun, then refilled the cartridge loops on his belt from the box of ammunition he kept in a saddle-bag. He checked the action of the pistol before holstering the weapon. Then he left the room. The hotel was quiet, and he went out to the street and walked through the shadows to the law office.

Roscoe Dayne was sitting behind the desk in the office, his feet resting on its top, his arms folded. He straightened up when Belmont walked in on him and his heavy features twisted into a frown.

'You got my prisoners safely behind bars?' Belmont asked.

'Sure thing.' Dayne motioned to a bunch of keys lying on a corner of the desk. 'You wanta check 'em out? There ain't anyone busting out of here while I'm on duty.'

'I want to find out why they were laying for Tilda Camford.' Belmont's eyes glinted as he studied the deputy's face. 'What can you tell me about the trouble goin' on around here? Who's causing it? Do you have any idea?'

'If we knew who was back of it we'd have done something about it,' Dayne countered. 'You figure we ain't on top of our job?'

'I don't figure anything at the moment. I need to learn about the situation and, being the local law, you should have some idea what's going on.'

'I leave all that to the sheriff.' Dayne shrugged his heavy shoulders, his face expressionless. 'Herb takes care of the county. I stick to handling this office.'

'And the town marshal? What about Goymer?'

'He's a good man.' Dayne spoke quickly, too quickly, Belmont suspected. 'There was shooting in the barn so he went in ready for trouble. You wasn't wearing your Ranger badge and Goymer figured you were up to no good. That's why he wasn't about to give you a chance.'

'So that's his story. Where is he now?'

'Sure I've talked to him. I needed to know what was going on. Goymer's got a shack just out of town, beyond the livery barn, and he's been taken there. He'll be out of action about three weeks, the doc says.'

Belmont picked up the cell keys and went through to where the prisoners were caged. The man he had shot in the livery barn was lying stretched out on a bunk, apparently asleep. The other, who had taken the kick in the head, was sitting on the foot of his bunk, shoulders hunched and his head in his hands.

He looked up at Belmont, scowled, then hurriedly dropped his gaze and refused to meet the Ranger's keen eyes.

'What's your name?' Belmont demanded.

'Names don't matter where I come from,' the man said harshly.

'So where do you come from? You've been around Broken Ridge about a week, so I heard. Where were you before that?'

'What's past is past.'

'You or your pard mentioned a man named Orton just before Tilda Camford and Baldy came into the barn,' Belmont persisted. 'Who is Orton? Is he the rancher at KO?'

'Never heard of Orton. Must have been him who mentioned the name.' The hardcase jerked a thumb at the unconscious figure in the next cell.

Belmont shook his head. 'If that's the way you wanta play it, then go right ahead.' He shrugged his heavy shoulders. 'But you should be aware that it won't get you anything but a long spell behind bars.'

He went back into the office to find Dayne riffling through the pages of the mail-order catalogue, and although the deputy looked up at him he did not stop turning the pages.

'Who's causing all the trouble in the county?' Belmont asked, and Dayne sighed heavily and threw down the catalogue. He looked at Belmont for several moments without speaking, evidently thinking over the situation. 'You know about the trouble, huh?' Belmont persisted. 'This ain't all news to you, is it?'

'Sure I know about it. But I don't know who the hell is back of it. If we knew that we'd do something about it.'

'So you said before.' Belmont moistened his lips. 'Tell me about Orton, Kane Orton.'

'How'd you drop on to that name?'

'One of the two prisoners mentioned it before the shooting started in the barn, and from what was said I figured they were working for Orton.'

'You better wait for the sheriff to get back and talk to him. He knows just about everything that happens in the county. Me, I just obey orders. I don't know a damn thing. All I do know is that the job is becoming too dangerous for what it pays.'

Belmont went to the door without a word and departed, mentally tagging Dayne as hostile. So he had to start his investigation elsewhere. He paused in the darkness of the street and glanced around. The town seemed quiet, but he was not fooled by appearances. Maybe he should quit now and get some sleep, then make a fresh start in the morning. After some deliberation he figured it was the best move he could make and walked through the shadows towards the hotel.

His thoughts were busy, and a number of questions were clamouring in his mind. Why had those two men been intent on kidnapping Tilda Camford? He toyed with the thought. Obviously someone wanted to put pressure on the girl's father, as she herself had stated. He considered the Bar C to be the most fruitful angle to pursue, and as there was nothing he could do on that line until daybreak he decided to call it a day.

The noise emanating from the saloon attracted his attention and he paused at the batwings and peered inside. The place was doing good business, with several card games being played at some small tables, and at least fifteen men were standing at the long bar.

He suddenly sensed that he had been approached silently from behind and, as he stiffened, a harsh voice spoke hoarsely at his shoulder, 'Don't turn around, mister, and keep your hands clear of your belt. I want a word with you.'

Belmont remained still, his breathing restrained. A cool breeze was blowing into town from the north but suddenly he was sweating. He sighed long and steadily, emptying his lungs of pent-up air and expelling the tension that was present in every muscle of his body.

'What's on your mind?' he demanded.

'I'm the deputy marshal of this town, buddy, and I just got word that you gunned down my boss, Sim Goymer.'

'Did you also hear that Goymer was intent on shooting me in the back?'

'Nope. But if he was gonna do that then he must have had a pretty good reason for it. You're a stranger in town. What's your business?'

'Who told you I shot Goymer?' Belmont countered.

'Why'd you wanta know?'

'Whoever it was didn't give you all the facts: he kept the most important bit to himself. I'm a Texas Ranger.'

'The hell you say!'

'So how does that sit with you?'

'It makes a big difference. I had you pegged for a hardcase, and we got too many of them around here as it is. Weren't you wearing your badge when Goymer got to you? He wouldn't have made his play if he'd known your business. Let's get off the street somewhere so we can talk. We need to thrash this out.'

'You lead the way.' Belmont was relieved when the man moved out from behind him and started along the street. He saw that the newcomer was not holding a gun and followed instantly. 'You got a name?' he asked.

'Frank Stoll. Goymer and me are about the only honest lawmen in the county.'

'I already got Dayne pegged as hostile, but what about the sheriff?'

'He's bogged down by the men who keep him in office.' Stoll was tall and heavily built. A star was glinting on his shirt front. 'I'm talking about the mayor, Pete Bainter, and his sidekicks on the town council. They're out to make fast bucks, and don't care much where they come from.'

'Sounds interesting. So the county law is crooked and the town law isn't.'

'You better believe it. I'm taking you to see Goymer, and he'll put you straight on the local set-up. Get off on the wrong foot around here and you're a dead man. The local hardcases play for keeps and the stakes are high.'

'How come there are so many lawmen around here but trouble is running wild?' Belmont dropped a hand to his holstered gun and eased the weapon slightly, feeling strangely uneasy. He wished now that he had questioned Baldy Jex more closely about the locals. He should have had a run-down on everyone connected with controlling the town. Baldy would have set him straight with the facts, for he knew without doubt that the ex-Ranger could be trusted.

'The sheriff don't handle the law inside of town limits,' Stoll said. 'Me and Goymer do that. And Dayne ain't really a lawman, although he wears a deputy badge. He's just a glorified jailer.'

'Had you heard that a Ranger was in town?' Belmont asked.

'Nope. Dayne kept that close to his vest. Just shows you the way county law is being handled. If you pay heed to anything Dayne tells you then you'll likely be dead come morning.'

They had reached the stable, and beyond the glare of light emanating from the lantern hanging above the wide doorway there was impenetrable darkness. Belmont halted, his hand dropping to his gun. He was not about to walk into trouble.

'The marshal's shack is about one hundred yards to the left, Stoll said. 'Get around the corner of the barn and you'll see the light in Goymer's window.'

'Lead the way, and take it slow,' Belmont told him.

'Sure thing.' Stoll moved forward.

Belmont followed closely, walking across the open doorway of the barn, his eyes narrowed against the glare of the overhead lantern. When he heard a faint sound coming from inside the stable he whirled instantly, but before he could get into action, a heavy object crashed against his head and he sprawled on the hard ground, falling instantly into a black, soundless pit which seemed to gape open at his feet and swallowed him entirely.

Three

Belmont's first intimation of returning consciousness was a throbbing pain in his head. Bright lamplight was pressing against his eyelids, and for some moments he resisted the temptation to open his eyes. When he stirred he discovered that he was unable to move, and realized that he was hogtied. It took an effort to open his eyes, and he had to blink against the light. He grimaced at the weight of throbbing pain hammering inside his skull.

When his eyes became accustomed to the light he looked around, the slight movement causing pain to shoot through his head. He was in a small room, lying on a dirt floor, and two men were playing cards at a table in a corner. Belmont tried to ease his cramped limbs, figuring that he had been tied for several hours. There was a window opposite, and black night was pressing in against the dusty panes.

'What's going on?' he demanded, and both men jerked around to look at him. 'Who are you, and why am I tied?'

'You're a mite too tough for the likes of us to handle,' one of the men replied, scowling. He was big, with a fleshy face and a broad nose that, at some time in the past, had been broken and badly set. His

37

face was half hidden behind an unkempt black beard, and his dark eyes glared balefully from under beetling brows.

'That's a fact.' The other was tall and thin with a sick-looking face. 'You put Hackett and Brewer out of action. But them two dummies ain't got an ounce of savvy between them. All they had to do was put down Baldy Jex and grab the Camford gal, and they sure made a mess of that. You stuck 'em in jail, and you plugged Goymer. That makes you a big nuisance to the boss, so you're on the way out before you can make any more trouble.'

'The boss sure ain't pleased, the way you walked into that trap in the barn and spoiled it,' the other observed. 'You're a dangerous man, Ranger, and we're hauling you outa here before dawn to plant you in the desert, where you belong.'

'It ain't wise to kill a Ranger,' Belmont observed.

'When it comes to doin' our job, we ain't got no sense at all.' The beard on the heavy face parted to reveal a thin-lipped mouth, and guttural laughter boomed across the shack. 'We're gonna plant you, Ranger, with any more of them long noses who show up. Now button your lip or you'll get another lump on your skull. We got some serious card-playing to do before we ride out. It's your deal, Jake.'

Belmont lapsed into silence, studying the hard faces of the two men. He closed his eyes, bothered by the glare of the lantern standing on the table. So where was Frank Stoll? Was the deputy town marshal also a victim of these hardcases, or had he been in cahoots with them? And Sim Goymer! It sounded as if the town marshal was playing a double game.

He must have lost his senses again, for suddenly he jerked awake to find the two men preparing to leave.

The darkness at the window had paled to grey. His head was still throbbing, and there seemed to be a great, painful weight inside his skull. He forced his mind to full alertness.

'It's about time we were riding,' one of the men observed. 'Crow should be here now with the horses. Where in hell is he? It'll be full light in another half-hour.'

Belmont flexed his muscles to test the rope binding him and realized that he could not hope to escape. He was securely hogtied. When there was a knock at the door he tensed, ready to take advantage of any chance that would enable him to outwit his captors. One of the men opened the door a crack and a harsh voice informed him that the horses were ready.

'About time, Crow, ' the man complained. 'Where in hell you been? It'll be full daylight before we get clear of town.'

'Cut the cackle and get him outa here pronto,' came the harsh retort.

Belmont was dragged to his feet, his hands still tied, and manhandled out of the shack. Dawn was breaking, although the town was still in deep shadow. There was a dim crimson glow on the eastern horizon, and the chill night breeze was warming up. Three horses were waiting with trailing reins and Belmont was thrust into a saddle. The man who had brought the animals sneaked away quickly and the two captors mounted. One of them led Belmont's horse, and he swayed in the saddle as they began to move out. His sense of balance seemed faulty, and he found it an effort to remain upright.

'You ornery galoots ain't going no place,' a harsh voice called from the shadows to Belmont's right.

'Drop your reins and lift your hands, yuh polecats, so I can see 'em, or I'll start shooting.'

Belmont jerked his head around and saw Baldy Jex step forward out of the shadows. The old ex-Ranger was holding a big pistol in his right hand and it was lined up unwaveringly on the two hardcases. The pair halted immediately. The bearded man lifted his hands without hesitation, but the other made a play for his pistol, lifting the weapon out of its holster as quick as the lick of a snake's tongue.

The gun in Baldy's hand blasted instantly and reddish flame spurted from the muzzle. The sound of the shot hammered out the silence and a string of raucous echoes chased away across the sleeping town. The hardcase dropped his gun and slumped in his saddle, causing the horse to shy. The animal cavorted a few steps, then stopped, and the man slid out of the saddle and thumped to the ground.

'That's better,' Baldy observed. 'It's about time you made a move outa that shack, you guys. I been watching the place ever since they dragged you inside, Clay. You ain't hurt none, are you, young feller?'

'Someone put me to sleep for a time and I woke up with a headache,' Belmont responded. 'I'm obliged to you, Baldy. They were figuring to bury me out in the desert.'

'I reckoned you'd need someone to watch your back until you got your teeth into this crooked business.' The old ex-Ranger laughed harshly, a cackling sound that echoed in the early morning. 'That's why I tailed you when you left the hotel. Good thing I got experience in such matters, huh? Now you get outa that saddle, Cassidy, and do it slow. Keep your hands away from your waist. I'd sure like an excuse to plug you.'

Baldy came forward as Cassidy dismounted and stood with his hands raised shoulder high.

'Shuck that hogleg and do it slow,' Baldy continued. 'Be careful. I'm a mite nervous this time of the morning.' He waited until the pistol thudded on the ground. 'Now untie Clay.'

Cassidy obeyed, and Belmont sighed with relief as the rope fell away from his wrists. He dismounted stiffly, head throbbing painfully and hands filled with excruciating cramp.

'What happened to my gun?' he demanded.

'In my waistband,' Cassidy growled, and Belmont stepped in close and relieved him of the weapon.

'You know this man. Baldy?' Belmont observed, as the ex-Ranger came to his side.

'Yeah. He's one of a dozen hardcases riding for Kane Orton, the guy who owns the KO ranch. The jigger I plugged is another of Orton's gun crew name of Jake Platt. The whole bunch of 'em have been riding roughshod around the range, trying to make big tracks. I been wanting to make 'em pull in their horns, but Asa, he's a stickler for the law, and he gived the sheriff too many chances to do it according to the law. But I figure that's all in the past now. Orton is in such a big hurry to get rid of you that his bunch have come into the open at last, much to my personal satisfaction. Now we can get to work on them, and there are some in the crooked bunch that I wanta take care of personal.'

'Do you know a man called Crow?' Belmont asked.

'Yeah.' Baldy chuckled. 'Crow is part Indian. Does odd jobs for Orton. He's over there in the alley, hogtied. I let him bring the horses in before I buffaloed him.'

'I'm beginning to believe the tall stories my pa

used to tell me about his early Ranger days,' Belmont observed.

Baldy chuckled. 'Son, you better believe them, and if you double everything Wild Bill told you, and then add a pinch more, you'll get nearer the mark of what really happened.'

'Did you see Frank Stoll drop on to me outside the saloon?' Belmont asked.

'Sure did.' Baldy cackled again. 'When these two busted you I watched until I knew where they brought you before I went after Stoll, who faded into the night when you dropped in the dust. He's been behind bars since around midnight. I know who's crooked around here, Clay, and you're gonna need me to give you a hand to clean up.'

'What about Goymer? Stoll said he was taking me to talk to the town marshal when he led me into that trap.'

'We can go talk to Goymer soon as we've put Cassidy and Platt behind bars. Goymer is working with Orton. You're gonna have your work cut out when you tangle with Orton's bunch, Clay.'

'I'll cross that river when I come to it,' Belmont replied. 'Let's get these hardcases to jail. If it keeps up like this there won't be enough cell space to house all my prisoners.'

Daylight was gradually filtering into the dusty corners of the still sleeping town. Belmont checked the fallen Jake Platt to discover that the man was dead. Baldy had planted a bullet in Platt's heart. Belmont felt a new respect for the ex-Ranger as they collected Crow from the alley and took him with Cassidy to the jail.

Roscoe Dayne was sitting behind the desk in the law office when Belmont and Baldy ushered in their prisoners. The deputy sheriff sighed heavily and got to his feet, reaching for the bunch of cell keys as he did so.

'Looks like this is gonna get to be a habit now you're in town,' he observed. 'What have you grabbed these two for? Still, I shouldn't ask that question, seeing who they are. I figure we'll hang Crow one of these days, and Cassidy has been throwing his weight around lately.'

'Hold 'em for assault until I can get around to them,' Belmont said. 'Right now we got things to handle before folks in town are awake.'

Dayne grinned. 'Stoll's been complaining about being on the wrong side of the bars.'

'Same charge for Stoll. And Goymer will be in here with him soon as we can get to him.' Baldy spoke grimly. Eagerness was lining every angle of his weathered face. 'Let's go grab him, Clay. You'll need to clean up in town before you think about moving out on the range.'

'You've sure picked yourself a tough chore,' Dayne said, 'but I've seen it coming, and I'll help you all I can, Ranger.'

'Thanks.' Belmont nodded his appreciation. 'If you keep my prisoners safe until I need 'em it'll be a big help.'

Baldy was already pushing the prisoners towards the cells, and Dayne chuckled as he unlocked the door leading to the cell block.

'Ain't Herb gonna get a big surprise when he comes back to town?' he remarked.

The prisoners were jailed and Baldy displayed eagerness to get after the crooked town marshal. Belmont was content to let the ex-Ranger take temporary control. The oldster knew who was crooked around town, and if they could jail the prominent badmen before the town awakened then they would have a head start in the bid to wrest control from those in power.

The sun was peering over the eastern horizon as they walked along the street, and already the heat of the coming day was packing in amongst the adobe buildings. Baldy glanced at Belmont and grinned. His leathery face was gaunt, his narrowed eyes looking strained from lack of sleep. Belmont felt a pang of warm regard for the oldster. Baldy had taken the plunge into this dangerous business, and looked set to clean out the town before breakfast. The old ex-Ranger was certainly still capable of law-dealing.

'Clay, you got to promise me one thing,' Baldy said. 'Don't let on to Tilda what's goin' on. She wouldn't like it one little bit if she knew I'm back on the clean-up trail. Heck, she didn't even want me to get myself a drink last night. You have to be real careful around she-males, son. They got strange notions about the way men should live. I ain't seen eye to eye with them on anything, not in a coon's age.'

Belmont smiled. They were passing the front entrance to the hotel and a sudden movement there caught his attention. Glancing sideways, he was ready to pull his gun but relaxed when he saw Tilda Camford emerging from the building. Baldy spotted the girl at the same time and groaned.

'There's never no peace when a woman's around!' he muttered.

'Morning, Clay,' the girl called. 'You're about early. And what dragged you out of bed at this time, Baldy? You haven't been out all night, drinking and gambling, have you? If you have then you ought to be ashamed of yourself.'

'No, ma'am, I sure ain't been doin' none of them things,' Baldy replied, and Belmont smiled when he considered the way they had both spent the night. 'Me and Clay are just taking a little walk. I got a bounden duty to help the law, and I'm just pointing out some of the local snags Clay might come up against when he starts law dealing around here. If you ain't had breakfast yet then you should tend to that right away. We need to be on the trail back to the ranch pretty soon now.'

He kept walking while he spoke, and Belmont was relieved when Tilda lifted a hand in acknowledgement and went back into the hotel.

When they passed the stable, Belmont saw a lone shack just beyond town limits. There was a saddle horse tethered to a post by the door of the ramshackle little building. Baldy dropped a hand to his holster when he saw the animal.

'Goymer's got a visitor already,' he observed. 'That hoss belongs to Muley Hogben, one of Kane Orton's gunnies. He's the bully of the bunch. Do you wanta wait until Goymer is alone, or make your move now, Clay? Hogben is built like a buffalo and handles himself like a one-man army.'

'If Goymer is crooked then most of his pards will be from the same mould,' Belmont assumed. 'Let's drop in on them now and see what's being cooked up for breakfast.'

'Hogben's hoss has been hard ridden,' Baldy observed, as they walked to the shack. 'You putting a slug through Goymer must have inconvenienced Orton some, I suspect. He relies on Goymer to use the town marshal's job as a buffer against the real law. Your arrival was well timed, Clay. We'll secure the town with little trouble if we put Goymer behind bars.'

'It seems to me half the town is crooked,' Belmont said softly.

Baldy chuckled. 'You could be right at that. But we just want the main ones right now. Most of your trouble will come out on the range, so you gotta knock the town into shape before you branch out. I reckon your job needs at least two men to handle it, Clay.'

'You and me, huh?' Belmont reached the shack just ahead of Baldy and drew his gun as he knocked on the door. Baldy had already palmed his pistol and, when the door was opened by a huge man dressed in range clothes, the old ex-Ranger grinned and levelled his weapon, pushing ahead of Belmont.

'Morning, Muley,' he greeted. 'Bet you ain't pleased to see me! Back up so we can see how Goymer is today. We got some of your pards in jail, and I figure you'd best come with us to see how they're doing. Lift your hands and I'll draw your fangs.'

The big man raised his hands without protest, his eyes flickering past Baldy to look at Belmont and then dropping to take in the Ranger badge on Belmont's shirt front. Baldy stretched out a long arm and jerked the man's pistol out of its holster. In that instant Muley Hogben moved with surprising speed for one of his massive bulk. He grabbed Baldy in a bear hug, pinioning the old man's arms to his sides. Baldy's gun clattered on the ground, and Belmont, still moving forward, side-stepped quickly to avoid a collision with both men. Hogben hurled Baldy bodily out of the doorway and slammed the door with tremendous force. Belmont was in the doorway, and took the impact on his left shoulder. He kept moving forward as the door flipped open again, entering the shack and swinging his gun barrel in a short arc to connect with Hogben's large head. The shock of the contact between gun and head sent a pain up the length of Belmont's arm, but Hogben merely shook his head, roared his defiance, and grasped Belmont's gun arm.

Belmont was three inches over six feet in height, but Hogben was half a head taller, and built like a Dutch barn. As pressure was applied to his right arm, Belmont kneed the big man in the groin, and Hogben grunted, immediately releasing his hold and jerking away before Belmont could follow up. Belmont realized that he had lost his grip on his gun and stepped in close, whirling his left fist in a vicious hook that took Hogben flush on the jaw.

Hogben staggered backwards on his heels and was brought up short by the far wall of the shack with an impact that threatened to dislodge the roof. Belmont followed up instantly, stepping in close and unleashing another left, aiming for the same spot on the giant's jaw. It was a battering blow that would have felled a buffalo, but Hogben merely shook his head and growled like a brown bear awakening from hibernation. He surged erect, shaking his head to throw off the effects of Belmont's heavy blows.

Belmont ducked the big man's lumbering attempt to apply a bear hug and whirled his shoulders, summoning up every ounce of strength and power. His left crashed against Hogben's jaw, halting the man in his tracks, and as Hogben's hands dropped to his sides, Belmont's right fist slammed in a tight loop against the left side of the big man's stubbled jaw. It was a battering blow that rocked Hogben's head back on his bull-like neck, and his immense body sagged helplessly, arms flailing, balance suddenly gone. He fell back against the wall behind him and slid down it heavily to lie in a gasping heap on the dirt floor.

'You'll be more comfortable in a cell, Goymer,' Baldy observed, and Belmont looked round to see the ex-Ranger standing on the threshold with his gun levelled at the town marshal lying on the bunk in a corner. Baldy wrinkled his nose and grimaced. 'This place smells like it's been housing skunks,' he observed. 'Get on your feet, Goymer, and move out. You ain't gonna let a little scratch keep you in that flea pit, are you? I thought you figured yourself to be all man. Hell, you ain't tough, you only smell strong!'

'What's goin' on?' Goymer demanded.

'You're under arrest.' Belmont was breathing hard. He massaged the knuckles on his right hand before retrieving his pistol from the floor. 'We're gonna have to wait until Hogben can walk,' he observed. 'There ain't no way we're gonna be able to carry him.'

Baldy chuckled. 'I don't figure the jail will be strong enough to hold him,' he retorted. 'We'll have to take extra precautions. You got a helluva punch, Clay. I ain't never seen Hogben put down before, let alone laid out cold.'

There was a pail of water standing on a small table, and Baldy picked it up, carried it to where Hogben was lying, and threw the contents into the big man's face. Hogben sat up, spluttering and cursing, and Belmont covered him with his gun.

Goymer was lying fully dressed on the bunk, and Baldy went to the town marshal and helped him to his feet. The man was tall and lean, with sharp features and narrowed, merciless dark eyes. There was a cruel twist to his thin lips as he gazed impassively at Belmont.

'You're the Ranger, huh?' he demanded. 'What for are you taking me in?'

'I got your measure,' Belmont said. 'Get him

moving, Baldy. We're wasting time. I'll ride herd on Hogben.'

'You ain't got no right to arrest me,' Hogben roared, clenching his big fists. 'I'll see you in hell before I walk into a cell.'

'Let's get something straight,' Belmont said. 'There are two ways you can go to jail: the easy way is to walk down there and let me lock you up; the hard way is for you to resist. I don't much care which way we do it. That's up to you. You got the choice. Just decide which way you wanta go and we'll get to it.'

Hogben gazed at Belmont, then lifted a great paw of a hand and massaged his jaw. Belmont waited, able to read the thoughts running slowly through the big man's brain. He grinned when the man shook his head slowly, finally deciding against action.

'You got the drop on me for now,' Hogben said, shaking his massive head. 'But you're gonna pay for this, Ranger. You ain't gonna be able to keep me in no jail, and when I get free the first thing I'll do is look you up.'

Belmont motioned with his gun and the big man staggered out of the shack. Baldy was ahead of him, supporting Goymer with his left arm and holding his pistol in his right hand. Belmont remained out of arm's length of Hogben as they walked towards the jail, and they were halfway along the deserted street when the clatter of many hooves sounded and a dozen riders came fast into town, raising dust.

'That's Orton's bunch,' Baldy flung at Belmont. 'Do we take 'em on or play it close to the vest?'

'There are too many for a stand-up fight,' Belmont said coolly, as the riders came up and circled them. 'Don't shoot unless they start it. I don't figure they'll take on the law in the open.'

'What's going on here?' The foremost rider, a man of around fifty, had the brusque manner of someone accustomed to being obeyed without question. He was wearing a light-blue store suit and a white Stetson, the brim of which was pulled down low over hard, questioning brown eyes. He was lean and looked to be in good physical condition for his age. A pearl-handled pistol was nestling in a black cartridge belt around his waist and his hand was close to the weapon. 'Talk to me, Jex,' he rapped. 'What are you doing with Goymer?' His gaze flickered to Hogben before fastening on Belmont, and his eyes narrowed when he spotted the Ranger badge on Belmont's shirt front.

'Figure it out for yourself, Orton,' Baldy replied. 'Ranger law has come to town. Meet Clay Belmont, the man who's gonna clean up Peso County, with me helping. We're starting with the small fry, but pretty soon we'll get around to the likes of you.'

'I ain't done nothing wrong, boss,' Hogben spluttered, waving his massive arms. 'I heard Goymer got hisself shot last night, and I was in his shack talking to him when these two busted in and arrested me. They dragged Goymer outa bed and figure to throw us both in jail.'

'What's the charge against Hogben?' Kane Orton stepped down from his saddle and trailed his reins.

'You can come along to the law office and hear what'll be said,' Belmont invited. 'And then you can tell me why some of your men took me prisoner last night, held me until dawn, and started out of town this morning with the intention of burying me in the desert.'

'Some of my men?' Orton shook his head firmly. 'I don't think so.'

'Cassidy and Crow, with Jake Platt, who got hisself killed for his trouble,' Baldy said harshly.

'The hell you say!' Orton's dark eyes met Belmont's keen gaze. 'Mebbe I will go with you to the jail at that. I'd sure like to know how some of my crew are mixed up in this without my knowledge.' He turned and glanced at his assembled riders. 'You men go get some breakfast, or something, and stay out of trouble. I'll get back to you shortly. Matt, take my horse, and keep the men quiet. You got that? I don't want trouble in town unless I start it.'

'Sure thing, boss.' A big, bearded man grinned as he came forward and grasped Orton's reins. He moved away along the street with the rest of the crew following, and Belmont noted the sullen manner of the whole outfit.

Belmont heaved a silent sigh of relief, but was not taken in by Orton's manner. Baldy seemed certain that Orton was bossing the trouble in the county, and the men who had given Belmont trouble during the night belonged to Orton's crew, but if the KO rancher was not giving the orders then the crooked business went a lot deeper than appearances suggested, and Belmont did not like the thought of what he would have to involve himself in to get at the truth.

Four

Roscoe Dayne was eating his breakfast at the desk when Belmont and Baldy ushered their prisoners into the law office. The big deputy's jaws stopped champing when he saw them and he dropped his fork with a clatter. Shaking his head, he got quickly to his feet, wiping his mouth on the back of his left hand.

'Two more prisoners for you, Roscoe,' Baldy said cheerfully. He glanced at the silent Kane Orton, who had followed them closely. 'Mebbe three,' he added, with a grin.

The deputy picked up the cell keys. 'I don't know what you're up to, Ranger,' he said. 'But if you can make any charges stick against these men then I'll hold 'em in jail.' His gaze flickered to the silent Kane Orton, who remained in the background. 'Are you under arrest, Mr Orton?' he queried.

'He ain't - yet!' Belmont glanced over his shoulder at the rancher's impassive face. 'I'll take your gun though, Orton. You'll get it back if I figure you have nothing to do with this business I'm looking into.'

Orton stood motionless for a moment, considering. Then he pulled his gun and held it out, butt first. 'I'd sure like to know what's going on,' he said.

52

'You've got some of my crew in the jug for breaking the law and it looks like you figure I gave them orders. Well that ain't the way of it. So let me see my men.'

Dayne led the way into the cell block, jangling his keys. Belmont dropped back to bring up the rear, gun in hand, and when Goymer and Hogben were locked behind bars he went to the door of the cell holding Cassidy and Crow. Both men were lounging on bunks, and neither changed his indolent positions when confronted.

'Orton, I told you what Cassidy and Platt said when they were holding me prisoner,' Belmont said. 'They figured to take me into the desert and plant me. Crow turned up with their horses, and if Baldy hadn't been watching my back I sure would be in a bad way right now. Both Platt and Cassidy mentioned their boss. That's you. So what gives here?'

Orton pushed close to the barred door of the cell. Crow was sitting on a bunk, his eyes downcast, ignoring their presence. The bearded Cassidy arose and came to the cell door, gripping the bars with big hands.

'You got it wrong, Ranger,' Cassidy said heavily, shaking his head. 'We got ourselves a riding job with KO so we could stick around the range. But Orton ain't our boss, and never was. We're working for someone else; using the KO outfit as a cover.'

'Then who are you working for?' Belmont demanded.

Cassidy grinned, still shaking his head. 'It ain't for me to say. Yuh gotta find that out for yourself. It's your job to stick your nose in where it ain't wanted.'

Belmont turned and walked back into the office and the others followed, Dayne pausing to lock the heavy connecting door before going back to his breakfast, jangling the cell keys. Orton faced Belmont with impassive face, his bleak eyes narrowed to the merest slits, then held out his hand.

'I'll take my gun,' he said. 'You heard what Cassidy said. They took a riding job with me so they could stick around on the range. There's been a lot of rustling lately, and you can bet they're mixed up in it. Go ahead and check 'em out. I'll give you any help you need. Call on me for anything.'

'Not so fast.' Belmont thumbed back the brim of his Stetson. 'Hogben is one of your crew and he drew on me the minute he saw me. And at the time he was visiting Goymer, who tried to shoot me in the back last night. Goymer is, or was, the town marshal, and his deputy, Stoll, led me into the trap set by Cassidy and Platt.'

'Hogben ain't been riding for me long.' Orton shook his head. 'It's obvious he's another using my spread as a cover for something else. So he was visiting Goymer. I guess that makes it obvious that Goymer and his sidekick have thrown in their lot with the rustlers.'

Belmont glanced at Baldy, who grimaced and shrugged his shoulders. Belmont reluctantly held out the gun he had taken off the KO rancher. Orton snatched the weapon, holstered it, then turned to the door.

'I ain't gonna rest until I've got to the bottom of this business,' he said, pausing in the entrance to look back at Belmont. 'There are others on my payroll I want to talk to, and if I find they're working for two bosses I'll bring 'em in for you to question. We've got big trouble on this range, and it looks like you'll have to dig a lot deeper to bring it to light.'

'Before you go,' Belmont said, 'tell me why you rode in this morning with a dozen of your crew?'

Orton grimaced. 'We're making an early start on some work I've got planned, and soon as the store is open we're picking up supplies and making for my northern line. I've figured that's the way the rustlers are taking my stolen stock off the range, and I mean to put a stop to them one way or another.'

The KO rancher departed and Baldy holstered his gun.

'I figured we got him cold,' the ex-Ranger declared. 'But though he's a slippery cuss I can't help figuring that somehow he's telling the truth. Cassidy could have been lying just now, Clay, and he sure got Orton off the hook. I think you better keep an open mind about this. I reckon the best thing we can do is grab some breakfast then head out to Bar C. Asa will need to talk to you, and between us we might come up with some answers to the questions bothering you right now.'

Belmont nodded. 'Sure,' he mused. 'I reckon there are more pointers you can give me when you've thought some more about the situation.' He looked at the attentive Dayne. 'Can you handle this office with all the extra guests in the cells?'

'Sure thing. You can go about your business without another thought to your prisoners. They're out of circulation, and they'll still be here when you come back. There's a couple of dependable men in town I can call on for help if I need it, and we'll take care of things.'

Belmont nodded and departed, his mind already tussling with other problems. He and Baldy walked along to the hotel and entered the dining-room where Tilda Camford was finishing her breakfast.

She smiled warmly as Belmont sat down opposite her.

'I shall be ready to ride out as soon as you two have eaten, she said. 'Did you enjoy your morning stroll?'

'It's too quiet around here this time of the morning,' Baldy responded, winking at Belmont. 'I was showing Clay the town. He needs to get his bearings fast. I'll be glad to get back to the ranch. I'll saddle your hoss soon as we're ready to split the breeze, Tilda, and bring it here to the hotel.'

The girl smiled. 'I'll be waiting in my room,' she said, and took her leave.

'Some folks don't know the half of what is going on around them,' Baldy said. 'But I wouldn't want anything bad happening to Tilda, Clay. I've knowed that gal from the day she was born, and, if I had to, I'd take to an early grave to stop the wind from blowing on her.'

'She'll be a whole lot safer back on Bar C with the crew around her,' Belmont said thoughtfully. 'Why was she being kidnapped last night? I reckon a tighter rein should be kept on her until this business is settled.' He looked around for the waitress and raised a hand to attract her attention. 'Let's get breakfast over with and hit the trail. I can't wait to meet Asa Camford.'

'He'll sure be surprised to meet you,' Baldy retorted. 'Him and your pa had something special going between them when we were Rangers. It was a pity Asa had a yen to be a rancher. Me and your pa handed in our badges to string along with Asa.'

'And you stuck with Asa. Why did my pa leave?'

'He had the law-dealing bug worse than me and Asa put together. He stuck with ranching for about a year, then took a deputy sheriff job over on the Pecos. We never saw him again. That's the way trails separate in life, huh? Then your pa met with your ma and they married and settled down.'

Belmont was silent as they ate breakfast, his thoughts dwelling on the past. He had inherited his father's passion for law dealing, and his one regret was that Wild Bill had not lived to see his only son follow in his footsteps.

After breakfast they went to the stable and saddled their horses. Then, while Baldy went to the hotel to fetch Tilda Camford, Belmont rode to the law office. Roscoe Dayne was seated in the office with his feet up on the desk, and Belmont wondered if the deputy ever did anything else. Dayne seemed to be glued to his chair. But the deputy grinned when Belmont walked in on him.

'You sure saddled me with a bunch of sidewinders,' he complained. 'Goymer is protesting his innocence at the top of his voice – or was until I threatened to shove his mattress in his mouth. And the others are asking to see the town lawyer. It looks like I'm the only man in town who likes the jail. But mebbe that's because I'm the only one on the right side of the bars.'

'Do you figure you can keep your prisoners locked up until I get back?' Belmont asked. 'I need to talk to Asa Camford and get the lie of the range in mind. I reckon to be gone two, mebbe three days.'

'The prisoners will still be inside if you're gone six months,' Dayne replied harshly. 'I ain't lost a prisoner yet, and I don't figure to start now.'

'There might be some pressure put on you when I leave town,' Belmont mused. 'Do you figure you can stand up to that? Kane Orton seems to be mighty determined, and if he's the man behind this trouble then I don't reckon he'll let the grass grow under his feet.'

'No one is gonna get my prisoners free no how,' Dayne said stubbornly.

Belmont nodded and departed to find Tilda and Baldy sitting their mounts at the hitching rail outside.

'You got through giving Dayne orders?' Baldy demanded.

'I didn't cotton to him when I first saw him, but I think he might just do what he's paid for,' Belmont replied.

'He's rough and ready, but I figure his heart is in the right place,' Baldy agreed. 'Mind you, before he took on the deputy job he looked like he was heading down the wrong trail. He drank and gambled and couldn't hold down a regular job. I never thought he could handle it, but he's better than most of the men who have tried lately.'

Belmont mounted and rode on Tilda's right while Baldy moved up on the girl's left. They cantered along the street, and Belmont's eyes were slitted as he watched their surroundings. Townsfolk were going about their morning business, but there seemed to be a silence lying over the town that struck Belmont as hostile.

They rode at a comfortable jog and the hours of the morning passed monotonously as they crossed the undulating range in a land that seemed devoid of habitations and other riders. In the distance to their left, a stretch of blue mountains shimmered in the heat-haze. The sun overhead was merciless, baking them with its harsh glare. They were silent for the most part, the heat heavy upon them, almost like a physical burden.

From time to time, Belmont glanced at the girl beside him, instinctively liking what he saw. He could feel a strange emotion unravelling in his breast, and clenched his teeth as he fought to prevent it taking hold. As a Ranger, he was not able to live a normal life, and that fact caused a gnawing sadness to occupy his thoughts. He could not side-step his duty for an instant. He had to remain single-minded, faithful to the oath he had sworn on joining the Rangers, and until now he'd had no yearning to live a normal, uneventful life.

The sun was past its zenith when they breasted a skyline and a valley opened out below them. Belmont reined in to obtain his first glimpse of the Bar C cattle ranch. Timbered ridges pushed up on the high slopes of the valley as if to conceal it from the eyes of passers-by, and Belmont nodded slowly as he looked out over vast space. The sun threw scintillating brilliance on the rippling surface of a stream meandering through the valley, the source of which lay in the distant mountains. The stream wandered close to a cluster of wooden buildings, widening into a shimmering creek before narrowing again to continue its natural way southwards.

'That's Bar C!' There was a catch in Tilda's voice when she spoke. 'Pa certainly knew what he was doing when he settled here.'

'If I'd saved my money like Asa did I'd have had a share in this place,' Baldy said without rancour. 'I never did have no sense, huh?' He chuckled as he gigged his mount forward. 'Let's get on down there and talk to Asa.'

As they neared the buildings, the sound of pounding hooves broke the silence, and when they rounded a corner of the long bunkhouse, Belmont saw a wrangler busting a horse in a corral at the edge of the wide yard. Dust was rising as the spirited animal tried to unseat its rider, and Baldy called out some advice to the ranny as they reined in at the corral. The rider came close to the poles and dismounted quickly, letting the horse prance away to the far side of the corral. He looked very young, and his slight figure did not seem equal to the task he was performing.

'Charley, give yourself a break and take care of these animals, will yuh?' Baldy called.

The youngster climbed on the fence and sat on the top pole, his expression serious. He was sweating profusely, and pushed back his Stetson to wipe his brow on a sleeve. He had very blue eyes and straw-coloured hair. His piercing gaze studied Belmont for a moment before he turned his attention to Tilda.

'You shouldn't've gone into town yesterday,' he said. 'You were told anything might happen.'

'Well nothing did,' Tilda responded, her lips pulling into a thin line.

'But there was trouble on the range,' Charley continued. 'Luke Wenn came in from the south range after midnight, carrying a bullet in his back and word that rustlers had hit the big herd. They got away with a coupla thousand head. Luke took on the bunch and collected a slug as he came home with the news. He died just before dawn this morning. The boss rode out at midnight with most of the crew and no one's come back yet. There's just a couple of us left to take care of the place. And I'm to tell you, Baldy, that you're to stay here with Miss Tilda and watch for trouble. You ain't to go out after the crew nohow.'

'The hell you say!' Baldy twisted in his saddle and looked around as if expecting a bunch of rustlers to come riding into the yard at that very moment. 'Tilda, get in the house and stay there. Leave your hoss here. We'll tend to that. Who else is on the spread, Charley? Asa left enough of you to hold the place, didn't he?'

'Just Jem Cleaver and me. Jem's up in the loft in the barn, watching the approaches.

'He didn't let rip when we rode in,' Baldy complained.

'He wouldn't because he knows you.'

'Yeah. And mebbe he's asleep up there. I'll go take a looksee.' Baldy dismounted and trailed his reins. He pulled a Winchester rifle from his saddle holster and checked the weapon. 'You keep your eyes skinned, Charley,' he said, as he kicked through the dust of the yard towards the barn. 'Come on, Clay, let's see what we got here, huh?'

Belmont dismounted and armed himself with his Winchester. He watched Tilda crossing the yard to the house, which was a hundred yards away, and had just started following Baldy, who was almost running towards the barn, when the sound of pounding hooves alerted him and he swung to face the wide gateway. A bunch of mounted men came hammering into the yard, raising dust in a billowing cloud.

At that moment, a rifle crackled from the barn, and Belmont saw the foremost of the riders throw up his arms before pitching from leather to disappear under the hooves of the following horses. Tilda started running back towards Belmont. Baldy had dropped to one knee and was already sighting his long gun on the riders.

Belmont heard shooting from the group of newcomers and slugs crackled about him. He dropped flat, working the mechanism of his rifle, and then all hell broke loose. Baldy was already hurling a stream of hot lead into the thick of the horsemen, and Belmont paused only to check that Tilda was down in cover before he turned his attention to the attackers. He began to work the lever of his rifle and the deadly weapon hurled slugs into the mass of oncoming men, some of whom were already falling into the dust under the concerted fire of Baldy and the man in the barn.

Belmont's accurate fire cut into the massed riders, and pandemonium spread as men were knocked out of their saddles, their horses whirling and crashing into others as the shooting took effect. Within seconds the survivors were pulling out, bent low in their saddles, six-guns clamouring as they fired and fled. Baldy got to his feet but continued shooting, and Belmont, holding his fire, saw two more riders pitch to the ground in testament to the old ex-Ranger's gun skill.

Five men were stretched out in the dust and three horses were down. Belmont's gaze was bleak as he looked around. The shooting had faded into the distance, and he could hear echoes grumbling away across the vast expanse of illimitable range. He saw the young cowboy, Charley, running across the yard to where Tilda was slowly getting to her feet. Baldy was reloading his rifle while staring after the escaping riders, his stiff lips moving jerkily as he silently cursed the troublemakers.

Baldy came towards Belmont, his leathery face set in harsh lines, but his eyes were glowing with excitement and grim pleasure.

'We showed 'em,' he said. 'Heck, it was just like the war! And if'n they hadn't turned tail we'd have dropped all of them. What for did they have to run?'

'More to the point, who are they and what did they want?' Belmont asked. 'Take a look at those we nailed and see if you can put names to them.'

'They'll be Orton's riders,' Baldy said instantly. 'I figure he's got two crews on his payroll – the men we know as KO riders, and those he pays to do the rustling.'

Belmont walked forward to the nearest of the fallen men and waited for Baldy to examine him.

'Dead,' the ex-Ranger observed. 'And I ain't never set eyes on him before. Orton ain't gonna risk getting caught by using men we could recognize.' He moved on to the next man, studied him for a moment, then shook his head and went on to the next. After looking at all five men he shook his head in irritation and frowned as he met Belmont's steady gaze.

'All strangers to me,' he said, heaving a long sigh. 'I'll check those other two over by the gateway, but I figure the answer will be the same. These men ain't known around here.'

'One of them is still alive,' Belmont said, eyes narrowed. 'Mebbe he'll talk after we've patched him up.'

Tilda came up, accompanied by the youthful cowboy. The girl's face was pale, her eyes wide in shock.

'Where did that bunch come from?' she demanded.' I've never seen so many strangers on the range.'

'I'll ride out and follow some tracks,' Belmont decided. 'I don't think that bunch will come back in a hurry. If they're working for Orton then I want to know about it.'

'I'd like to ride with you,' Baldy said immediately, 'but I can't leave Tilda here with just two men. Asa would skin me alive if I pulled a trick like that.'

'I can handle it alone,' Belmont said softly. 'See you when I get back.'

'Don't take any chances out there.' Baldy spoke worriedly. 'Why don't you wait for Asa to get back? Then you can have half-a-dozen men riding at your back.'

'I got a job to do, and if headquarters didn't think I could handle it alone they would have sent another man with me.' Belmont smiled and went back to his horse. He slid his Winchester into its boot and mounted easily. For a moment he sat looking around, then shook his reins and sent his mount towards the gate. He lifted a hand to Baldy and the girl, then continued, pausing once to stare intently at the massed tracks in the dust left by the unknown riders who had been intent on murder.

The riders had headed south, and Belmont wished he had seen a map of the range in order to orientate himself. But he didn't need to know the way to any of the neighbouring ranches; all he had to do was follow tracks.

Six horses were leaving prints on the range, and they were riding fast. Belmont pushed his horse into a canter and followed easily, his gaze lifting frequently to study the rough ground ahead. He had to be prepared for ambush, and kept his right hand close to the butt of his holstered six-gun.

He was five miles from the Bar C, when he topped a rise and saw his quarry about a mile away, riding easily, jogging along as if they did not have a care in the world. Belmont pulled back behind the rise and dismounted, trailing his reins when the horse was below the skyline. He dropped flat and peered over the crest to watch the progress of the riders. Was he still on Bar C range? He had no way of knowing.

When the riders had passed out of sight, he arose with the intention of going back to his horse and riding on, but there was a rider coming up the slope towards him from behind, holding a six-gun in his right hand, the muzzle of which was aimed unerringly at Belmont's chest.

'Just stand still and keep your hands away from your belt,' the stranger called. 'I got a keen interest in galoots acting suspiciously on this range.'

Belmont remained motionless, eyes narrowed and watchful. The stranger was tall, gaunt and thin, and had a long, angular face that looked as if it had been roughly fashioned with a small axe. He was dressed in a dusty store suit, and an old, badly weathered Stetson was pulled low over his piercing brown eyes. He reined up a couple of yards from where Belmont was standing and stared at him with harsh gaze.

'Who are you, and what's your business?' he demanded. 'You're acting mighty suspicious, mister, else I can't tell a jackass from an elephant. What are you doin' on Bar C range?'

'What I get paid for,' Belmont replied.

'And what's that? Rustling? Who are you spying on?'

'A bunch of men who rode into Bar C earlier and started shooting up the place. I'm Clay Belmont, Texas Ranger. Now it's your turn, mister. Who are you, and why are you riding around with a gun in your hand?'

'Where's your law badge. It should be on your chest where everyone can see it.'

'I don't wear it on the range. It makes too good a target.'

'I have the same trouble,' the newcomer grinned, and lowered his gun. He pulled aside his jacket and revealed a sheriff's badge pinned to his shirt on the left breast. 'I'm Herb Grant, sheriff of Peso County. My office is in Broken Ridge. I had word from Ranger Headquarters that you'd be riding in any time. Glad to know you, Belmont. You need any help then just say the word. Have you been in Broken Ridge?'

'Left town this morning.' Belmont reached into a breast pocket, produced his Ranger badge and pinned it to his shirt front.

Sheriff Grant holstered his gun and dismounted. He came to Belmont, hand outstretched. He was as tall as the Ranger. They shook hands.

'Did my deputy offer you any help?' the sheriff asked.

'Sure thing. He's holding some prisoners I turned over to him.' Belmont explained tersely the events that had taken place in Broken Ridge and the sheriff nodded slowly.

'I had some business over Valverde way so I ain't been around for a couple of weeks, but from what you've told me I figure the cat is coming out of the bag. There's been trouble around here for a long time and it's deep rooted. I got Orton and his KO outfit pegged as being behind the trouble. But it's widespread, and there's no telling just what is going on. So you plugged Sim Goymer, huh? It's a pity you didn't kill him. He's a crooked galoot if ever I saw one. I don't know how he got the job of town marshal.'

'I need to get on,' Belmont interrupted. 'I'm on the trail of half-a-dozen hardcases and I wanta run them down.'

'I figure you can handle that chore with no trouble,' Grant nodded. 'I gotta make tracks for town.

From what you say I've been away too long. I'll work with you, Belmont, should you need any help.'

'Thanks.' Belmont went to his horse and swung into the saddle. He lifted a hand to the sheriff and rode on over the ridge to follow the tracks heading south. When he glanced back over his shoulder just before losing himself beyond the ridge, it was to see the sheriff heading in the general direction of the distant town. Then he saw something else which made him rein in and seek cover. A rider had appeared from a gully to the sheriff's left and the two men converged swiftly.

Belmont saw the sheriff twist in his saddle and look over his shoulder, but Belmont was hidden from his gaze. Herb Grant dismounted and spoke seriously to the newcomer, turning to point out the direction Belmont was following. Belmont frowned as the newcomer drew his pistol and checked the weapon. Then he lifted a hand to the county lawman and came at a fast clip along the tracks Belmont had left.

Belmont turned his horse and rode on, wondering if the sheriff had sent the man to help or stop him. The county lawman had not made a good impression on Belmont, and, with the experience of years of Ranger-work behind him, Belmont was not about to take anything for granted. He would presume that every man was against him until it was proved otherwise.

Five

Belmont rode at a canter to make up the ground he had lost on his quarry, and watched his back-trail intently, disturbed by the knowledge that a stranger was behind him. But he failed to spot any sign of the man who had started to trail him, and guessed the newcomer was taking care to remain concealed. He crossed another ridge and moved below the skyline before dismounting and crawling back to the crest. Minutes later, he saw the stranger coming forward steadily and watching the ground intently for tracks.

Continuing, Belmont was grim-faced as he pushed on to get closer to the six men he was following. But half his concentration was focused on the man behind him, and he soon realized that he could not do full justice to his duty with a big question mark against the man on his back-trail. Crossing yet another ridge, he left his horse out of sight and went back to the crest. When the man arrived minutes later, Belmont drew his gun and pushed himself to his feet.

The newcomer reined in swiftly, but made no hostile move towards his holstered six-gun. He was tall and lean, in his late thirties, Belmont surmised. His low-brimmed Stetson was pulled down over his forehead, shading his narrowed eyes from the glare of the sun, and he remained motionless in his saddle, content to let Belmont take the initiative.

'You're playing a dangerous game,' Belmont said harshly. 'You're just asking to get shot, trailing me the way you're doing. I saw you talking to the sheriff back there. What's your business?'

'Herb Grant asked me to keep an eye on you.' The man shrugged his wide shoulders. 'He reckoned you've got a tough chore on your plate and figured I could help out should you find it too much to handle. I'm Jake McGruder. I got a little cow spread west of here and I've been sounding off lately about the lack of law and order in this county. Herb figured I should take a hand in the showdown that's coming, and that's how come I'm riding on your tail.'

'I work alone, and up to now I haven't found a job that's been too tough for me to handle.' Belmont's tone was harsh.

'There's always a first time.' McGruder pushed back the brim of his Stetson and wiped beaded sweat from his forehead. 'Sure is hot,' he observed. 'You got any objection to me tagging along with you for a spell, at least until you come up with that bunch you're trailing?'

'Yeah. I object,' Belmont nodded. 'I'm playing this as it comes and I don't need any distractions. I don't want to havc to watch out for you as well as myself, so when you depart I'll get on with it.'

McGruder shrugged, and for a moment a faint smile showed on his thin lips. 'I ain't never been a man to stick his nose in where it ain't wanted,' he said, 'but Herb Grant mentioned that Bar C was hit by a hard bunch last night, and if these tracks you're following belong to some of those hardcases you'll be knee-deep in trouble when you catch up with them. I'd like to tag along and help out if needed.'

'While we're gabbing about it they're putting more distance between us,' Belmont said sharply. 'Light out, McGruder. I don't need wet-nursing.'

McGruder shook his reins and wheeled his horse to his left. Belmont sat motionless, missing nothing, and waited until the man was cantering back the way he had come. Perhaps McGruder was on the level, but this was not the time or the place to take chances with anyone. Belmont returned to his horse and swung into the saddle. He rode back to the crest and studied his back-trail; McGruder had already crossed a ridge and was out of sight. Belmont shook his head and resumed the trail.

The sheriff had not made a favourable impression on him when they met, Belmont realized. There had been an indefinable something in the local lawman's manner that had grated on the senses, and he rode on thoughtfully, examining his impressions closely, looking for pointers that might aid him in his task. While he rode, he maintained his high level of alertness, and twice reined aside and dismounted to study his back-trail. Finally he was satisfied that McGruder had departed, for he saw no further sign of the rancher, and began to push on faster, following the riders who had galloped into Bar C and started shooting.

The tracks were so clear and easy to follow, Belmont did not like it. This was too easy. The riders ahead of him were aware that they could be tracked, and he moved carefully, ready to quit his saddle at the first sign of trouble. An ambush was now a grim possibility and his nerves were greatly overstretched as he anticipated the first hammering impact of questing lead striking his flesh.

Hitting a long slope, he was halfway to the crest when a rifle hammered out the heavy silence and a bullet crackled in his left ear. But he had seen a slight movement ahead as the ambusher sighted his rifle, and was in the act of quitting his saddle when the shot rang out. Clawing his Winchester from its scabbard, he went sideways, and hit the ground hard and rolled into a nearby depression on the slope before a second shot could be fired at him. His horse turned instantly and went down the slope several yards before halting and standing with trailing reins.

The ambusher fired a string of shots that dusted Belmont's position, and he remained low and motionless. A slug tugged at the crown of his hat and he removed it and waited out the leaden storm that raged around him. Rolling on to his back, he jacked a cartridge into the chamber of his rifle and waited patiently for a chance to use the long gun.

Pounding hooves nearby warned him that developments were taking place. He risked a glance up the slope to see three riders coming down at him on an angle, while the rifleman on the crest poured an acurate stream of covering fire into Belmont's position. Ducking, he waited out the seemingly endless moments, and when the riders were too close for the ambusher to keep firing, Belmont eased himself upwards a fraction and lifted his long gun into the aim, his eyes narrowed against the glare of the brilliant sunlight. Sweat was trickling down his bronzed forehead.

The riders had spread out, putting space between them, and now they were only yards away. They began shooting with six-guns, and Belmont compressed his lips as he bought into the action. He triggered the Winchester, hardly seeming to aim, but each shot claimed a hit. The foremost rider jerked back in his saddle as if he had ridden into the side of a mountain. His six-gun spilled from suddenly nerveless fingers and he pitched sideways out of his saddle to thump lifelessly on the hard slope.

A bullet nicked Belmont's left thigh and he jerked as if he had been touched by a hot branding iron. He shifted his aim, swinging the muzzle of the rifle to the left, and fired at the man who had shot him. His bullet took the hardcase through the centre of the chest and the man fell sideways out of his saddle. Twisting to bring the third man under his muzzle, Belmont clenched his teeth when he saw the man drawing a bead on him, but at that moment a bullet struck the hardcase in the upper chest and his gun fell from his limp hand.

Belmont glanced to the right and was surprised to see Jake McGruder coming fast up the slope, gunsmoke drifting around him. The rancher fired again, aiming at a target on the crest, and Belmont turned his attention in the same direction. He saw a fourth man on the skyline in the act of moving back, and sent a couple of shots upwards to hurry him. The man full forward from view and Belmont ceased firing.

The shooting faded then and echoes grumbled away to the distant horizon. Belmont pushed back the brim of his Stetson and looked around quickly to take stock of the situation. He was sweating profusely. There was pain in his his left thigh just above the knee. He got to his feet, taking his weight off his injured leg as he checked his surroundings. He saw McGruder coming up fast, and the man's teeth flashed as he grinned.

'Good thing I kept coming along behind you,

huh?' he demanded, as he reined up in front of Belmont.

'I had it under control,' Belmont responded tensely, then relaxed and grinned. 'Thanks anyway. It sure was tight for a coupla moments.' He glanced along the crest, saw no signs of trouble, and dropped to the ground to examine his wound.

'I'll take a look around while you doctor yourself,' McGruder said, and touched spurs to his mount and went on up the slope.

Belmont heaved a long sigh and put down his rifle. He saw a bloodstained bullet hole in the left leg of his pants and reached for his knife. Slitting open the soaked cloth a couple of inches, he found a long gouge in his flesh on the outside of the thigh, and was relieved that the bone had not been touched. The wound was not serious. He removed his neckchief, shook out the dust, and got up and limped to where his horse was standing patiently. Soaking the neckerchief with water from his canteen, he applied it to the wound and tied it tightly. Then he was ready to get back to duty.

McGruder was coming back down the slope, grinning widely, and dismounted when he reached Belmont. 'Two of them pulled out to the south-west,' he reported. 'There were six of them, huh? Looks like they figured it would be easy to take care of you. Anyway, they're sure fanning the breeze now. I doubt if we'll catch up with them this side of the border.' He trailed his reins and looked around, then walked to the nearest of the four downed riders.

Belmont accompanied him, wanting identification of the badmen. McGruder bent over the man and studied the inert features before straightening.

'He's dead, and he's a stranger. It's a funny thing,

but there's a mess of strangers riding the range these days. That's a bad sign, huh?'

'It's a sign that someone is bringing in hardcases to handle some dirty work,' Belmont said. 'Has there been any bad trouble around here recently? Real bad stuff, I mean? I know something is going on because I was sent here, but it looks as if I arrived as it started coming out into the open. Bar C was hit by rustlers last night, and a bunch of riders came into the Bar C yard just after I got there this morning, shooting and helling around.'

'It's been threatening to bust loose for a long time,' McGruder said. He checked the second of the three men and shook his head in response to Belmont's silent enquiry. 'This one is dead as well, and he's another I ain't set eyes on before.' He approached the third man, who was lying in a huddle on his left side, and rolled him over on to his back: sightless eyes gazed up at the brilliant sky. McGruder reached into a breast pocket for the makings and rolled a brown-paper cigarette while squatting over the body. He offered the tobacco to Belmont, who declined.

'You run a small spread, you told me,' Belmont said softly. 'Have you been bothered by rustlers?'

'They wouldn't bother with small ranchers.' McGruder shook his head and straightened, dribbling blue smoke from his flared nostrils as he went to the fourth man. 'You said rustlers hit Bar C last night? Asa Camford has reported losing cows lately but nothing much, and Kane Orton, who owns the big KO spread, has been complaining for some time that he's losing stock. Looks like you got here just in time, huh? It's beginning to bust loose.'

McGruder checked the fourth man and shook his

head as he straightened. 'There wasn't enough time for wounding shots,' he said. 'These jaspers were shooting for keeps. They sure meant to put you away, Ranger. But it's a pity we didn't get one of them alive. We might have got something useful out of him. How's your leg? Can you go on?'

'The leg will do. Would you take these dead men into town and make a report to the county law? I got to push on after the other two hardcases, and I've lost a lot of time as it is.'

'You better get your leg checked out by the doc in town,' McGruder opined. 'Those things can turn mighty bad in a short time. Why don't you take the bodies in?'

'It's my job to keep going while I can.' Belmont looked around. 'And I'm still wasting time.' He went to his horse and swung into the saddle. His leg was hurting but he ignored the discomfort and started up the slope.

McGruder stood for a moment, gazing after him, then shook his head and stepped up into his saddle. He moved up to Belmont's side and they ascended the slope to the crest. Belmont paused and checked the ground. Tracks were plain to see, and he pushed his mount into a canter and began to follow them. The sun was high in the faultless blue of the sky, and he judged the time to be around noon. There was still plenty of daylight left for his job.

McGruder stuck by his side and Belmont made no further attempt to get rid of the man. They rode in silence for more than an hour before McGruder twisted in his saddle and looked off to the right.

'We ain't far from Bill Halfnight's place now,' he said. 'Mebbe we better stop off there and get some grub while we can. This looks like it's gonna be a long job. Those hard cases ain't gonna stop for anyone.'

'I got supplies for a few days, ' Belmont replied, shaking his head. 'I'll keep going, and I'd better split the breeze for a spell. Can you tell me what lies in the direction these tracks are heading? These men I'm following have been riding steadily south or south-west and I reckon they must have a definite goal in mind. I've got to stick with them.'

'Kane Orton's spread lies about twenty miles from here, in the direction those galoots are riding. Have you learned anything of the situation that exists here in Peso County?'

'I been picking up bits and pieces since I rode into Broken Ridge. But I need to get a complete picture before I can work out what's going on. You better stop by the Halfnight spread and check that the hardcases didn't ride in there looking for trouble. I'll push on. You can follow my tracks if you need me.'

McGruder nodded and wheeled his mount away. Belmont kept an eye on the man's progress until he was out of sight but his full attention was on the faint trail he was following. These tracks were the only link he had with the trouble breaking out in Peso County.

The two sets of prints went on and on, and Belmont began to think that the riders were making for the Mexican border. Then he topped a ridge and reined in to look around, and stiffened when he saw a horse standing with trailing reins some 200 yards ahead. There was the motionless figure of a man lying on the grass beside the horse.

Belmont narrowed his eyes as he checked the surrounding range. There was a small herd of cattle off to the right but no sign of riders. He gigged his horse forward, drawing and cocking his six-gun as he neared the standing horse. He watched the man on the ground but saw no movement. When he drew nearer he noted that the man was lying on his face, as if he had pitched out of his saddle, and there was a patch of blood between his shoulder blades.

Belmont dismounted slowly and stooped to check out the man. A sigh escaped him when he found no sign of life. He looked into a gaunt, stubbled face of someone aged about thirty years, and it belonged to a man he did not know. As he straightened, his mind filled with innumerable questions.

He saw two sets of tracks continuing to the southwest and nodded slowly. This man was not a part of the fight at the ambush spot. He swung back into his saddle and rode on, aware that the odds against him were decreasing all the time. But he needed a prisoner who could be questioned, and went on at a faster clip, fired with fresh determination to come up with the men he was following.

An hour later, he breasted a rise and reined in swiftly, for a dozen riders were coming in his general direction, moving fast and raising dust. He dropped his gaze to the ground and saw the two sets of tracks he was following heading off to the left to a nearby stand of timber. He sat motionless as the riders came hammering up to him, and sunlight glinted on several drawn guns amongst the crew.

Kane Orton was leading the group, and the KO rancher reined in a yard or so in front of Belmont, who sat motionless, his face impassive and his manner matter of fact. He recognized some of the harsh faces of the riders, having seen them in town with the KO rancher earlier that morning.

'This is a surprise,' Orton said harshly. His smooth face was set in grim lines and his eyes held a bleakness that warned Belmont bad things were happening on the range. 'I lost a big herd of cows last night, Ranger. Have you seen anything of them?'

'When did you find out about that?' Belmont demanded. 'You were in Broken Ridge early this morning intending to do something about your northern line, so you said.'

'You're sitting on my north boundary right here.' Orton pushed back the brim of his weathered Stetson with an impatient thumb. 'One of my riders was waiting to tell me about the rustling when we arrived from town, and we just spotted a couple of riders out this way who shouldn't be on my grass. We were riding to pick them up when you came over the ridge on their tails.'

'I've been following those two men since this morning,' Belmont said, 'and there were six of them when I first took up their trail.' He eased his stiff shoulders as he narrated the incidents that had occurred since the shooting in the Bar C yard. 'By the sound of it there's more than one gang of rustlers at work in this county.' He went on to explain briefly about the raid on Bar C.

Orton shook his head and his expression hardened. He threw a glance at his men, who had grouped together at his back.

'Well, what are you waiting for?' he snarled. 'You saw those two men ride off when they spotted us. And you heard the Ranger say he's been tracking them all morning. Go get 'em, and bring 'em back alive. We need some answers from them thieving galoots. Snap, you and Mike stay with me.' He looked at Belmont and grinned harshly. 'You can forget about those two you were following. We'll take care of them.'

'I want them alive,' Belmont responded. 'I'll need to hear what they got to say about the rustling at Bar C.'

'Sure.' Orton grimaced as his riders went off fast in a cloud of dust. 'I got a line shack half a mile from here. If you've been trailing coyotes all morning then you'll be ready for a bite to eat and some coffee, huh? We can leave my men to pick up that pair. Ride along with me, Ranger.'

'Sure thing. Thanks.' Belmont never knew when he would get the opportunity to eat and drink on the range, and this seemed like a good time to rest up. He sided Orton and they cantered back the way the KO rancher had come, followed by two of the riders. Pretty soon a line cabin showed up on the bank of a small creek, and Belmont noticed two horses standing hip-shot in a small corral to the rear.

'You lost stock before this latest raid, I heard,' Belmont said as they dismounted and put their horses in the corral. He unsaddled his mount and the animal immediately stuck its nose into a water trough just inside the gate. He put his saddle on the corral fence.

'I've been hit pretty hard,' Orton admitted. His face was harshly set and his eyes glittered as he met Belmont's impassive gaze. 'There's organized rustling in the county on a large scale, but I ain't gonna take any more of it.'

'How come you ain't got together with the other ranchers to fight this thing?' Belmont asked.

Orton suppressed a sigh. 'You think I ain't tried? Hell, it's got so a man can't trust his neighbours any more.'

'Surely you can trust Bar C! Asa Camford and Baldy Jex are ex-Rangers. And they've been losing plenty cattle.'

'Some of my stock have been taken across Bar C range.' Orton shook his head. 'I ain't accused Camford of stealing my cows, but they sure as hell disappeared in his direction.'

'I learned this morning that rustlers hit the Bar C's north range last night around midnight. You say you lost cows from around here about the same time. From what I know of rustlers the same bunch couldn't have hit both herds, so there's either one big gang working in groups to empty the range or there are two different gangs working the same range. What do you think about that?'

'I don't know what to think any more.' Orton shook his head, and turned towards the line shack when a voice called his name.

'Hey, boss, did you get a line on them rustlers?' A cowboy was peering from the doorway of the shack. He was holding a rifle in his hands and the muzzle was lined up on Belmont's tall figure. 'Is this one of those two galoots who took off when they saw the outfit?'

'No, Cal. This here is a Texas Ranger. Come on out and say howdy. Tell him what you saw last night when some more of our cows went missing.'

Belmont, watching the newcomer closely, saw the man's heavy face stiffen at the mention of Texas Ranger, and the muzzle of the rifle did not move from its aim on Belmont's chest.

'This is Cal Snark,' Orton continued. 'He's been a great help on this northern line. Figures to know how rustlers operate, and he's been able to stop a couple of raids on my beef.'

Belmont studied Snark's face as the man came towards him, tight-lipped, snub-nosed, tall and thin;

dressed in black batwing chaps and a black leather vest over a pale-blue shirt. Snark's eyes were narrowed and bleak, and there was a small, jagged scar on his left cheek which stretched down to the corner of his tight mouth.

'So we got the Rangers on the job at last, huh?' Snark came to stand at Orton's side, keeping the muzzle of his rifle pointed at Belmont's chest. He looked quite casual and at ease, but Belmont saw signs of stress in the man's manner.

Belmont reached out a long arm and pushed the muzzle of the weapon away. Snark grinned as he lowered the long gun but there was no amusement in his narrowed gaze, only wariness, and he did not blink as he watched Belmont's impassive face.

'Sorry,' he said. 'It's got so a man cain't be too careful around strangers these days. Have you found any of the rustlers yet?'

'At least seven have been killed since a bunch of them rode into Bar C this morning.' Belmont wanted to shake Snark's confidence, and saw the man's cold eyes narrow still further. Snark was wearing a holstered six-gun on his right hip, and the weapon was thonged down for a fast draw. He had all the earmarks of a gunhand, and Belmont could only wonder why he was holding down an ordinary riding job.

'The hell you say!' Surprise touched Snark's tone. 'Nobody ain't seen hide or hair of any rustlers around here. Sounds like you had a big stroke of luck, Ranger.'

'The outfit is chasing two riders the Ranger has been trailing,' Orton said. He turned and canted his head to listen when the popping of gunfire rattled in the distance back where Belmont had halted in his trailing of the two hardcases.

'I hope your men will take those two rustlers alive,' Belmont said harshly.

'Don't worry about it.' Orton smiled grimly. 'I can trust my men to do what I tell them.'

'I did hear that you might be responsible for the rustling in this county.' Belmont spoke in an even tone, and saw a thin smile tug at Orton's mouth. He waited for the rancher's reaction, before hitting him with a shock, but Orton remained impassive, his mind enmeshed in local affairs.

'I reckon you must have been told that more than once,' Orton said. 'I know I've blamed just about every other cattleman in the county since this trouble started, so I figure the innocent ones must be doing the same with me.'

Belmont nodded, sensing that Orton was telling the truth. 'I believe you for the moment, ' he said softly. 'So tell me, how come you have a known rustler on your payroll?'

Orton froze at Belmont's words, but Cal Snark uttered a curse and whipped up the muzzle of his rifle. Belmont, hair-triggered for action and expecting it, stepped forward a half pace, his left arm swinging out, blocking the movement of the rifle, and at the same time he set himself to throw a punch. His right fist flashed in a short arc and his heavy knuckles crashed against Snark's chin before the man could drop his rifle and reach for his holstered six-gun.

Orton gasped in surprise and stepped back out of the way as Snark pitched sideways and fell senseless to the ground. Belmont eased back a couple of paces, drawing his six-gun with the speed of a rattler's strike, but as he cocked the weapon, a gun crashed in the background and a bullet breathed on his face. He dropped to one knee and swung his ready muzzle into the direction from which the shot had come. A man was emerging from the line shack, a smoking Colt in his hand.

The man lifted his gun as if to fire again, and Belmont tensed. But Orton uttered a livid curse and quickly stepped in front of Belmont, lifting both hands as he faced the newcomer.

'Hold your fire, yuh danged fool, Benny!' Orton yelled. 'This man is a Texas Ranger.'

'It's open season on Texas Rangers in this county,' Belmont said, getting to his feet and covering the approaching man, who now held his gun down at his side at arm's length, its muzzle pointing harmlessly at the ground. He glanced down at Snark, saw that the man was unconscious, and bent and scooped up Snark's discarded rifle. He jerked the man's six-gun from its holster and threw it several yards away. Then he faced Kane Orton and the newcomer, wanting an explanation, which, he hoped, would solve some of the questions facing him.

Six

'What's this about?' Orton demanded, staring at Belmont. 'How come you took a dislike to Snark?'

'It's more than dislike.' Belmont covered the newcomer as he halted beside the rancher. 'Drop your gun, mister,' he rapped. 'You don't get a second shot at me.'

The cowpoke, squat and heavily built, opened his hand and allowed his gun to fall to the ground. 'Heck,' he said. 'I looked out the shack as Snark made his play and figured you was one of them rustlers we're all fired up about.'

'Forget that, Benny,' Orton cut in. 'What was it you said about Snark, Ranger? You called him a rustler. Do you know him from someplace?'

'I've seen a description of him, and when you called his name I remembered hearing about him down Alverde way. He was running with a bunch of wideloopers I helped to put behind bars, but he lit out before I could take him. So he made tracks in this direction, huh?'

'He's been riding for me about six weeks, and saved my stock more than once.' Orton shook his head in disbelief. 'He's a rustler? No wonder he knew so much about the way rustlers work.'

'He was probably setting you up for a big steal,' Belmont observed. 'That's the way cattle thieves work these days. Has he got any pards riding for you? There could be more of these crooked galoots on your payroll. Rustlers are pretty well organized now. They cover everything. Nothing is left to chance.'

'Snark rode into the ranch one evening with Pete Davis. They was looking for riding jobs. I never had any reason to doubt their honesty, and they have worked hard for their pay.' Orton grimaced. 'Are you sure about this? I'd hate to lose Snark. Like I said, he saved my stock a couple of times. He sure knew about the way rustlers work.'

'Once a rustler always a rustler, so he had to be setting you up,' Belmont decided. He walked to where his saddle was lying on the corral fence and opened a saddle-bag to produce a pair of handcuffs. Snark stirred as the bracelets were snapped around his wrists, and Belmont stepped back, smiling his satisfaction as the rustler opened his eyes.

At that moment the rattle of approaching hooves attracted their attention and Belmont turned to face the bunch of riders cantering towards them, his right hand resting lightly on the butt of his holstered gun. Five riders were coming in and one of them was roped to his saddle. Dust spread as the riders reined up.

'We got one of those sidewinders,' the leader of Orton's men reported. 'Him and his pard showed fight but we convinced this one that he didn't stand a chance. The rest of the boys are chasing the other one. They'll bring him in when they catch him.'

'Does anyone know that one,' Belmont asked, studying the rider roped to his saddle. The man, big and capable-looking, with a vicious expression on his weathered face, was a stranger to him, he was certain, for he never forgot a face.

'Seen him around Broken Ridge more than once,' someone said. 'And he was always in the company of hard cases.'

'Who is Pete Davis?' Belmont persisted, and a man sitting his mount beside the prisoner stiffened and dropped a hand to his right hip, where a six-gun nestled in a cutaway holster.

'Raise your hands, ' Belmont ordered. 'I got your pard Snark dead to rights as a rustler, and as you're his sidekick I want to question you.'

Davis sat for a moment as if undecided about his next action. He looked at Snark still lying in the dust, shook his head slowly and lifted his hands in token of surrender. One of Orton's cowpokes leaned sideways and snatched the man's six-gun from its holster. Belmont, meanwhile, was making an effort to conceal his surprise, for he knew Pete Davis as Sam Bartleman, a range detective who had worked for the Cattleman's Association for years. Concluding that Bartleman was at present working under cover, he gave no sign of recognition.

Orton went to Davis and dragged him out of his saddle. He swung his left fist and crashed his hard knuckles against the man's jaw. Davis sagged, and Orton held him upright.

'I took you and Snark in and gave you good jobs,' he snarled. 'Now it seems you're rustlers. What have you got to say for yourself, Davis?'

'I ain't a rustler,' Davis protested, sagging to the ground when Orton released him. 'I ain't never been a rustler. I met Snark on the range just before I reached KO.'

'You came riding into my spread with Snark, who

is a known rustler,' Orton raged. 'In my book that
tars you with the same brush, Davis. You been biting
the hand that fed you.'

'I ain't put a foot wrong since I've been on this
range,' Snark cut in harshly, head shaking as he came
to. 'That's the truth, boss. I'd made up my mind to go
straight before I met Davis on the trail. We were on the
up and up when we rode into KO looking for jobs.'

Orton shook his head. 'I don't know what to think
any more.' He turned to Belmont. 'What you planning to do, Ranger? You got Snark dead to rights if
you say he's wanted for rustling. So I'll go along with
that. You must know what you're talking about, and
you're the only decent law we got round here. I don't
trust any of that bunch in Broken Ridge. You better
take Davis in with you and check him out. If he ain't
a rustler then he can still ride for me. Now what
about this galoot?' He looked at the prisoner his men
had brought in. 'You were with the bunch that rode
into Bar C earlier today, huh? One of that bunch
shooting and helling around.'

'He's one of them, ' Belmont said, when the man
did not reply. 'I recognize him.'

'We oughta hang him on the nearest cottonwood,'
Orton observed, nodding his head vigorously, 'and
leave him be as a warning to others of his kind.'

'I'll take him along with Snark and Davis into
Broken Ridge,' Belmont said firmly. 'The law will
deal with them. Davis will be released if there's no
evidence against him. Mebbe now we'll get some
information about what is going on around here.'

'Keep an eye on them, boys,' Orton told his men.
'We'll get coffee and some grub, Ranger. And you
can have a couple of my men to ride into town with
you when you're ready to go.'

Belmont was keen now to hit the trail with his prisoners, but he had not eaten in many hours and knew it would be as many again before he found an opportunity to feed himself. He followed Orton into the line shack, where the smell of cooked food tantalized his hunger. A man was busy cooking, and within minutes Belmont was sitting at a table and filling his empty stomach with good, well-cooked food. He relaxed slightly for the first time in many hours, and tried to get his thoughts working on the situation facing him.

Orton remained silent until they had eaten their fill. The rancher looked like a man who had a lot on his mind. Belmont stoked himself with enough food to keep going through the coming hours, and drank plenty of coffee before getting to his feet.

'Thanks for the grub.' He met Orton's level gaze and wondered at the rancher's thoughts. 'I'd better be on my way,' he added. 'It'll be dark before I reach town.'

'It ain't so far going back,' Orton told him. 'You went out to Bar C before coming on here, and that's a big half-circle. I'll send a couple of men back with you. They'll show you the quickest way to Broken Ridge.'

When they left the shack it was to find Snark, Davis and the third man roped to their horses in readiness for the trip to town. Belmont saddled up and prepared to ride and, as he swung into leather, someone called out that the rest of the riders were coming in. Belmont looked around, and his lips pulled tight when he saw that one of the newcomers was lying face down across his saddle.

'We got him but he didn't want to come along without a fight,' one of the cowpokes said grimly. 'He wasn't satisfied until we put a coupla slugs in him. Some fellers you just can't convince to give up.'

'Does anyone know him?' Belmont asked, and heads were shaken as he looked around.

'Jim,' Orton said, you and Fred can ride along with the Ranger. He needs to hit town soon as he can. Make sure he gets there with his prisoners, huh? And keep your eyes open for trouble on the way. Anything can happen now the rustlers are coming into the open.'

'Sure thing, boss.' A tall, thin ranny with a youthful face lifted a hand in acknowledgement and turned and grinned at an older man who kneed his horse forward a couple of steps. 'Looks like we been nominated, Fred,' he observed.

'It'll make a change from hunting rustlers,' Fred replied.

'And no hanging around town when you get there,' Orton warned. 'See the Ranger into the law office with his prisoners and then hoof it straight back here. You got that?'

Both men nodded and Orton faced Belmont, looking genuinely worried. Belmont could decide nothing about the rancher.

'I expect you'll keep me informed of what happens after this,' Orton said.

'You can count on it.' Belmont nodded. 'Thanks for your help, and for the food.'

'My pleasure.' Orton shook his head. 'I hope you can put this trouble to rights. It's creating bad blood and suspicion right through the range.'

Belmont nodded his agreement and rode out considering what he had been told about Kane Orton. He found it difficult to reconcile the information with reality. But he was accustomed to keeping an open mind, and his thoughts raced with conjecture as he followed the two KO riders, who were leading the three prisoners and the dead man.

Belmont rode in beside the prisoner who had been captured by Orton's cowpokes. The man was middle-aged, coarse-looking, with shifty eyes and a stubbled face. There was a hard expression on his features.

'I got you dead to rights, mister,' Belmont said harshly. 'I saw you with the bunch that rode into Bar C this morning. You took a hand in the shooting.'

'You can't prove that,' the man replied sullenly.

'I recognize the horse you're riding.' Belmont smiled. 'In my job it's easier to remember horses than men. You almost put a slug through me, and you'd be dead now if one of your pards hadn't crossed my line of fire as I threw down on you.'

'So I got a charmed life,' the man shrugged. 'You'll get nothing outa me. You're wasting your time.'

'What's your name?' Belmont persisted.

'If my mother gave me one when I was born then I was too young to remember it.' The man chuckled harshly, and Belmont dropped back a couple of paces, his attention turning to Pete Davis.

'Davis,' he called, and the range detective twisted in his saddle to look back over his shoulder. 'Drop back here. I wanta talk to you. Let's see if you can convince me that you ain't a rustler.'

The KO rider who was leading Davis released the short rope he had tied to the bridle of Davis's horse, and the range detective, his hands tied behind his back, allowed his mount to slow until Belmont reached his side. Belmont checked his horse until the others drew ahead out of earshot.

'Howdy, Sam,' he said. 'I'm glad to see you at work

in this neck of the woods. Can you tell me what's going on?'

'I haven't got the rights of it yet. Everyone is playing this game with their cards close to their chests. But I figure things ain't what they seem to be.'

'I already decided that.' Belmont grimaced. 'It's about the only thing I have. I heard in town that Orton is running the rustling, but I don't get that feeling, judging from what I've seen so far.'

'I still don't know if Orton is involved, and I've been riding this range nearly two months now.' Bartleman shook his head. 'Sometimes I get the feeling that Orton must know what's going on, but then the facts point some other way. All I do know is that we've got the biggest rustling deal ever building up on this range. And the rustlers are beginning to come out into the open.'

'I've only just come into the county' – Belmont twisted in his saddle and checked their back-trail – 'and I found trouble in Broken Ridge soon as I rode in.' He gave Bartleman a brief account of what had happened.

'You always did have the knack of getting straight down to business,' Bartleman grinned. 'Pity you didn't kill Goymer when you shot him. I suspect he's mixed up in the rustling somewhere. He's been down on me from the moment I hit this range. I think he suspects me of being connected with the law. But talking of Goymer brings me to Muley Hogben.'

'Yeah? What about him? I arrested him in town early this morning and threw him in the hoosegow.'

'The best thing you can do is keep him there.' Bartleman rasped the fingers of his left hand across the black stubble on his chin. 'There's something about the set-up betweeen Orton and Hogben that don't seem straight. I never saw a man and his boss act the way they do. At times it seems as if Hogben is running things. No ranny ever spoke to a rancher like Hogben does. And Hogben ain't got ordinary chores like the rest of us. He ain't never done a good day's work since I been on the spread.'

'So how does it add up to you?' Belmont pressed. 'Have you got anything in mind?'

'It seems to me that Hogben has got some kind of hold over Orton that gets him off normal chores. I can't put my finger on anything specific, but something definitely grates.'

'I heard in Broken Ridge that Orton knows about the rustling. So could Hogben be running that side of things for him while he remains outside it?'

'Mebbe you've hit the nail on the head.' Bartleman shook his head slowly, thinking deeply. 'Hogben is away from the ranch a lot. He's always being sent off somewhere on some minor errand. It sure looks to me like he comes and goes as he pleases. I'd like to be able to tail Hogben when he rides out. But I never get the chance. What I might have to do is lose the job with Orton so I can concentrate on Hogben's activities.'

'I'll question Hogben when I get back to town,' Belmont said. 'Now what can you tell me about Sheriff Grant?' He pushed back his Stetson, wiped his damp forehead on a sleeve, then eased his aching back and jerked the brim of his hat back over his keen eyes. 'I don't cotton to him. What kind of a lawman is he?'

'I don't rate him high. But I ain't got any evidence that he's on the take. Mind you, a bunch of the businessmen in Broken Ridge could be bossing the rustling. There's talk around town which I picked up pretty quick, but I ain't found anything solid to put a finger on. I've even considered that perhaps there are two rustler gangs here working independently of each other.'

'Exactly what have you learned? Have you got proof against any of Orton's bunch?'

Bartleman shook his head. 'Hogben gets my vote that he's mixed up in the rustling, but who the rustlers with him are is another thing. I'm sure they ain't all on Orton's payroll. I've seen one or two men around who are known to me as rustlers. And you've already found out that Hogben is thick with Goymer. That' s what makes me suspect Goymer. I also knew Snark is a rustler, so I played along with him when we rode into the OK spread to learn what I could. But he's been playing his cards close to the vest. He ain't trusted me from the start, and I'm sure he ain't made illegal contact with any of Orton's regular crew.'

Belmont cast his mind back to the incident with Hogben at Goymer's shack. 'If the deputy sheriff in town can be trusted, then Hogben will still be in jail when we get there,' he said. 'Do you want to ride in with me or go on working undercover?'

'I'd like to go on working for Orton a little longer. I might be on the point of breaking through.'

'And you won't be able to do anything if you're behind bars,' Belmont observed.

'That's right. So it looks like I'll have to escape from you before we hit town.' Bartleman looked rueful.

'I can make it easy for you. All I have to say is that I don't suspect you and you can go right back to Orton. Would that do?'

'I got nothing to lose,' Bartleman nodded. 'I need

to keep on the case now it looks like busting open. I can do more good out there on the range than hanging around town. The rustlers can't keep their activities secret for much longer.'

'OK.' Belmont reined in and unfastened the rope around the range detective's wrists. 'You're free to go, Sam. If you need to contact me leave a message at Bar C. I suppose Asa Camford and Baldy Jex are above suspicion, seeing they're ex-Rangers.'

'You're right. Have you got a spare six-gun I can borrow? Orton kept mine, and I don't like riding unarmed.'

Belmont opened a saddle-bag and produced a spare gun and a box of cartridges. Bartleman checked the weapon and grinned.

'Thanks,' he said. 'See you around, Clay.' He swung his horse and set off at angle to the trail Belmont was following.

Belmont watched the range detective until Bartleman had vanished over a nearby ridge. Then he rode on. The two KO men were riding steadily with the prisoners, and Belmont galloped his horse to catch them. They swung round at his arrival.

'Heck, you've lost Davis,' said the younger of the two.

'I don't lose prisoners,' Belmont replied. 'I turned him loose. There's no evidence of rustling against him. You've all been riding with Snark so if Davis is guilty of rustling then the rest of you could be. I can always pick up Davis if I should need him. Let's push on a bit, huh? I need to get to town fast.'

They continued, and Belmont was pleased with the way events were shaping. With Sam Bartleman working undercover the weight of the investigation would be halved. Now he had plenty to work on but needed to talk with Asa Camford as soon as possible to get the rancher's opinion of local trouble.

The sound of hooves on their back-trail roused Belmont from his thoughts and he dropped a hand to his gun as he glanced over his shoulder. A rider was galloping towards them. He told the KO men to keep going with the prisoners and reined up, turning his horse to face the newcomer. In a moment he recognized Jake McGruder.

'You're making good time,' McGruder said, as he halted in front of Belmont. 'I rode to Orton's line shack and he told me what had happened. I was following you when I was overhauled by Baldy Jex. He said Tilda Camford had disappeared from Bar C. She had insisted on riding to find her father, and sneaked away. Baldy didn't miss her for a coupla hours. When he did take out after her he found tracks that suggested she had been grabbed by a couple of riders who headed in the same direction as the men you were following. I left Baldy tracking them and came after you. Baldy figured you would want to be in on this.'

Belmont glanced around at his prisoners.

McGruder nodded. 'Orton told me what happened. I'll ride to town with this bunch if you wanta take out after Baldy.'

'Did you tell Orton about the girl?' Belmont queried.

'Yeah, but he figured it was Camford's problem. Orton's got enough on his plate without getting side-tracked, so he said.'

'Why would anyone wanta kidnap that girl?' Belmont mused. 'There was an attempt in town to take her, which I blocked. I can't believe rustlers would grab her without good reason. Are they trying to put pressure on Camford? But what would be the point? They're lifting Bar C cattle anyway. Is there something going on here that I don't know about? I've got to be missing something somewhere along the line. You're a local man, McGruder, what do you make of it?'

'It beats me.' McGruder shook his head. 'I've never heard of rustlers doing anything but lifting cows. But whatever the reason, I reckon Baldy Jex will need help to get the girl back. If you wanta take out after Baldy you'll find the trail well blazed. I figured to make it easy for you. Just ride back to Orton's line cabin, then follow my tracks. Baldy came up with me near the spot where you met up with Orton and his bunch. I read the sign. Just cut to the right from that spot and you'll pick up Baldy's tracks. He's following three horses, one of which is Tilda Camford's.'

'Thanks.' Belmont wheeled his mount and set off at a gallop back the way he had come. The rustlers could wait. If Tilda had been kidnapped then there was a much deeper game than mere rustling being played in Peso County and he needed to be in on it as soon as possible.

Reaching Orton's line cabin, he received a surprise, for there was only the cook at the place. Orton and his men had ridden out.

'I don't know where they've gone,' the cook told him. 'All I know is I got to have a meal ready for the crew at sundown.'

Belmont rode out, and soon reached the spot where he had met up with Orton. He saw the tracks heading left where the men he had been following most of the morning turned away, and when he checked right he found three fresh sets of tracks heading west, followed by a single set left by Baldy

Jex. He went on at a canter, aware that Baldy had been moving fast when he made the tracks. He pushed the horse into a gallop to make up time, and an hour passed before he heard the sound of shooting in the distance.

His eyes narrowed at the grim sound and he spurred his horse into further effort. The range ahead was sparse, its undulations thickly covered with brush. He kept to the seemingly never-ending line of tracks as he covered the rough ground. He counted at least three rifles firing, and eased his horse when he caught the pungent smell of gunsmoke on the breeze. He needed surprise on his side now.

Reining in on a crest, he slid out of his saddle to lead the horse back off the skyline, then jerked his Winchester from its scabbard. He dropped flat and bellied up to the crest, and the first thing he saw was Baldy Jex's horse lying apparently dead a hundred yards down the long slope before him. A man was crouched in a small depression not far from the fallen horse, and gunsmoke drifted as he fired sporadically at the opposite high ground, where two rifles were firing from cover and effectively pinning him in his depression.

Belmont hurried back to his horse and took his field-glasses from a saddle-bag. Once again in position, he soon saw that the lone man was Baldy Jex, and swung his glasses to check the opposite high ground. The two men up there pinning Baldy down were easy to see, and he quickly eased back into full cover and returned to his horse, ready to take part in the action.

He rode to the right in a wide half-circle, remaining concealed as he headed for the rear of the men's position. When he judged himself to be well clear of them he angled left and moved cautiously, ascending a slope and pausing on the edge of a narrow shelf backing the high ground where the men were positioned.

Belmont moistened his lips when he saw three horses standing in the brush, tethered to the lower branches of a lone tree. He dismounted, took his rifle, and left his horse with trailing reins, quickly heading for the three horses. One of the animals he recognized as Tilda Camford's, and then saw the girl seated on a low outcrop of rock near the horses. She was tied hand and foot.

Sneaking in, his attention on the area where the two men were still shooting, Belmont reached the girl and saw her start of surprise when she spotted him. She opened her mouth to cry out, but he held up a hand, motioning her to silence. He passed her by and went on up to the crest where the two men were lying in cover.

When he spotted one of the men, he dropped to his hands and knees and crawled forward, and the first thing the man knew of being stalked was when Belmont pressed the muzzle of his rifle against his neck. The man froze in the act of reloading and Belmont reached down and jerked the rifle out of his hands. He dragged a six-gun out of the man's holster and slammed the butt of his own rifle against the man's skull.

The man slumped into unconsciousness and Belmont arose, careful to remain out of Baldy Jex's line of fire. The second rifle was firing only a few yards further along the crest. Belmont strode forward. He saw the man in the act of firing yet another shot at Baldy's position and, as the gun echoes fled through space, the man caught Belmont's slight movement and glanced in his direction.

'Drop the gun and lift your hands,' Belmont called.

The man was at a disadvantage and froze, and Belmont went in close and kicked him in the head, then bent and dragged the rifle from his slack grip. The echoes of the shooting began to fade, and Belmont cautiously exposed himself on the skyline, yelling to Baldy Jex. The old ex-Ranger quickly accepted the changed situation and emerged from cover as Belmont stood up and waved to him.

Belmont secured his prisoners before going back to where Tilda Camford was sitting, now hoping that something of the true situation would be revealed to him by this rapid development of events.

Seven

Tilda Camford was looking happier than when Belmont first saw her, and the girl unleashed a torrent of questions when he returned to her side. Ignoring her interrogation, he untied her, his alertness undiminished as he awaited Baldy's arrival. The girl was overjoyed at being freed, and Belmont shook his head as he turned his attention to her.

'Why did you leave Bar C alone?' he demanded. 'I took the trouble to see you home safely and, although you knew someone was trying to kidnap you, you rode out alone and played right into the hands of the badmen. I was on my way to town with some suspected rustlers when I got word that you'd gone missing, and I had to leave my prisoners to come looking for you.'

'I wanted to talk to my father so I rode out to find him,' she said fiercely. 'I won't let the trail scum in this county keep me from doing what I want.' Her tone faltered then and fear showed momentarily in her eyes. 'But two men ambushed me near the ranch; evidently they were awaiting such an opportunity.'

'And you made it easy for them.' Belmont spoke

firmly. He heard Baldy Jex coming up the slope and went to meet the old ex-Ranger.

'I couldn't believe my eyes when I spotted you up here,' Baldy said, grinning. 'Did you kill them pole-cats, Clay?'

'No. Let's tie them. Then tell me if you know them. It's getting to the point where I need some proof, and fast.'

Baldy didn't need a second invitation. He went to the nearer of the two men, who was stirring, and quickly bound the man's wrists with a thong that was dangling from his holster. Belmont moved on to the second man, who was still unconscious, and tied him securely.

'This one I've seen around town,' Baldy said, standing over the man he had tied. 'And what do you think? He was on right friendly terms with Sim Goymer. I seen them drinking together in town more than once.' He toed the kidnapper with a dusty boot. 'What's your handle, mister? What kind of a game are you playing? It's a bad business, taking a woman off her home range against her will. I reckon Asa Camford will wanta string you up from the nearest tree when he gets to hear about it.'

'We didn't mean the gal no harm, 'the man responded. 'We was asked to take her off for a spell, that's all.'

'So someone could put pressure on her father, huh?' Baldy reloaded his six-gun. 'So how about trying to make things easy for yourself by giving us the lowdown? You're in a whole lotta trouble, mister, and there's only one way out of it. Talk. Tell us about it.'

'It's more than my life is worth.' The man shook his head determinedly. 'If I spill the beans I'll be heading down the trail to Hell soon as the boss finds out about it.'

'Who is your boss?' Baldy demanded harshly, but the badman did not reply.

'Are you mixed up with the rustlers?' Belmont asked, and the man sneered as he shook his head.

'Heck, I ain't a no-good thief! I got some principles. I make a livin' with my gun.'

But you ain't above kidnapping a girl,' Baldy mused. 'Now ain't that something? So you ain't worried about having to swing for what you've done.'

'I'll never come to trial,' the man retorted confidently.

Belmont walked across to the second man, who was beginning to stir, and grasped his shoulders and hauled him into a sitting position. The man held his head between his hands and uttered a low groan.

'You've got off pretty light so far, ' Belmont told him, 'but this is where the game turns bad for you. Why did you kidnap Tilda Camford?'

'To keep her outa the way for a few days. We wasn't gonna hurt her none.'

'Who paid you to do the job?'

'I ain't about to tell you that.' The man shook his head. 'We got well paid to do the job, and we'll take anything that comes our way.'

Belmont straightened, certain he would learn nothing from these hardcases. He turned to Baldy.

'I'll take these two into Broken Ridge,' he said. 'You better head back to Bar C in case Asa Camford has returned there. There's no telling what he'll do if he thinks his daughter has been kidnapped.'

'I ain't got a hoss,' Baldy said. 'They killed mine.'

'Take one of theirs. They can ride double until I get to Orton's line shack. There'll be a spare mount there. Push these two up on one mount, Baldy, and I'll have another try at getting to town.'

'Mebbe we should all ride together,' Baldy suggested. 'I wouldn't wanta walk into some more trouble, just me and Tilda. Someone is out to get hold of that gal so I figure to ride into town with you. Is that all right with you?'

'Yeah.' Belmont suppressed a sigh. 'But we'll have to split the breeze some. I got a lot of lost time to make up so let's get moving.'

The two prisoners were roped to a horse and they were soon ready to ride. Belmont fixed a rope to the bridle of the horse carrying double and led it as he pushed his own mount into a canter. Baldy and Tilda Camford followed behind, and they rode at a fast canter, back the way Belmont had trailed them.

When they reached the Orton line shack they picked up an extra horse, and made faster time afterwards. Baldy moved out ahead and took a short cut. The afternoon passed quickly, and as the sun disappeared behind the western horizon they topped a rise and Belmont saw the lights of Broken Ridge twinkling in the distance.

'We've made better time than I figured we could!' he exclaimed. 'I wonder if McGruder has arrived yet with my prisoners?'

'What do you make of McGruder, Clay?' Baldy demanded.

'Seems a decent enough young feller.' Belmont shook his head. 'But I guess I'll have to see which way he finally jumps before I make a decision on him. And that's the way I feel about most of the folks I've met in this neck of the woods.'

They rode down a long decline, but, as the minutes passed, the lights of the town did not appear to get any closer. Belmont fought down his impatience, his mind struggling with all the small facts he had gathered since his arrival in the county, aware that so far he had not gained anything really constructive.

It took them another two hours to reach Broken Ridge, and Belmont felt hung over with weariness when they reined up in front of the livery barn. There was a lantern hanging in the big open doorway, and he dropped his hand to the butt of his six-gun as he led his horse into the barn, forcing himself to ignore the brilliance. If there was another trap awaiting him then he would walk right into it, for it was time he did something drastic.

He left the two kidnappers tied to their mounts while they put their horses in stalls and took care of them. Belmont slung his saddle-bags from his left shoulder as they went back out to the darkened street, and he took hold of the reins of the waiting horses.

'I spotted McGruder's horse in a stall,' Baldy said. 'It looks like your prisoners have arrived.'

'I'm wondering now about the prisoners I left in jail when we left town early this morning,' Belmont mused. 'Do you figure Roscoe Dayne can be trusted?'

'It's too late now to worry about that,' Baldy chuckled. 'Let's see Tilda safely into the hotel and then we can take a stroll down to the jail and check up.'

'I want to stay with you,' the girl protested. 'I need to find out what's going on. Twice I've almost been kidnapped, and I can't figure out why rustlers would want to take me. It can't be to put pressure on my pa. Heck, they're stealing his cows anyway, and that's all they're interested in. They're getting what they want so why bother with me?'

'There's got to be another reason why they wanted to take you,' Belmont said, 'and I figure you're right to want to stay by me until we find out what that reason is.'

He led the two horses along the street and Tilda and Baldy walked along the sidewalk. As he passed the saloon, Baldy looked in over the batwings, then uttered an exclamation and halted.

'Hey, Clay, come and take a look-see in here,' he called.

Belmont wrapped the reins he was holding around a hitch-rail and crossed the sidewalk to the batwings of the saloon. Peering inside, his blue eyes narrowed when he saw Muley Hogben at the bar, talking loudly and waving his arms. He was in the company of three tough-looking men. Belmont noted that the big man was armed with a holstered six-gun.

'Do you still figure Roscoe Dayne can be trusted?' Baldy demanded at Belmont's side. 'Someone's let that big galoot out of jail.'

'Stay out here and watch my prisoners,' Belmont said through his teeth. 'I'll fetch Hogben back to the jail.'

'Sure, if you figure you can handle him and them others alone,' Baldy said doubtfully. 'That's a tough bunch he's got with him.'

'I'll take him,' Belmont said harshly. He eased his gun in its holster and thrust through the batwings.

Silence fell swiftly inside the saloon, and men looked at Belmont's tall, grim figure as he paused on the threshold. It took Hogben several moments to become aware of his presence, but eventually he glanced towards the door, and his blustering voice cut off in mid-sentence.

'I left you in jail when I rode out of town this morning,' Belmont said icily. 'So who let you out?'

'Mason, the lawyer, got me out. He reckons there ain't nothing I can be charged with. ' A sulky note sounded in Hogben's rough voice, and his right hand moved slowly towards the butt of his holstered gun.

'If you keep moving that hand you'll need more than a lawyer to get you out of the next place I'll send you, ' Belmont rasped, and the big man stayed his hand, remaining silent although his expression hardened.

'You figure you make big tracks, huh?' he demanded.

'Too big for you.' Belmont compressed his lips. 'Undo your gunbelt and let it fall to the floor. I'm taking you back to the jail so I can check your story. I arrested you this morning for assaulting Baldy Jex and attacking me, and you should be in jail until you've been before the judge. So let's go, mister. Get rid of your hardware.'

'I ain't going back to jail,' Hogben said flatly, and Belmont knew by the tone of the man's voice that he would not change his mind.

'Well, you got a choice,' he said. 'If you were turned loose by the lawyer then all you got to do is go with me to the jail and prove it. If you decide to resist I'll probably kill you, so if you figure it's worth dying for then go ahead and make your play.'

Hogben looked as if he would prefer to resist, and Belmont was hair-triggered to flow into action at the first sign of trouble. But one of the men beside Hogben reached out and grasped the big man's right arm.

'Don't be a fool, Muley,' he said. 'That man's a

Texas Ranger. You can't win nohow if you go up against him. Kill him and before you know it there'll be a dozen more of them law hellions riding in here. If you was turned loose this morning by Mason then you got nothing to lose. Go along to the jail and get it done right.'

Hogben exhaled heavily in a long sigh, his eyes glinting as he eyed Belmont. Then he shrugged. 'Sure,' he said, grinning. 'If that's the way you want it, Ranger, then that's the way it'll be.' He unbuckled his gunbelt and let it fall to the sawdusted floor.

'Step forward,' Belmont ordered, drawing his gun with a slick movement that was not overlooked by the watching men. 'I've had a hard day so let's get this done the easy way.'

'You'll be the one to look the fool when you talk to the sheriff,' Hogben said. 'Come on, I'm wanting to see this.'

He walked to the batwings and Belmont slid to one side to remain out of arm's length. Hogben shouldered his way through the batwings with such force that the doors smashed back at Belmont as he followed. Belmont took the shock of them without pausing and followed the big man out to the sidewalk, expecting Hogben to turn and attack him. But the man kept moving forward, and Belmont sighed in relief as he followed, his gun aimed at Hogben's broad back.

'I'll bring the prisoners along, Clay,' Baldy said, and Tilda came out of the shadows to walk at Belmont's side.

The street was shrouded in darkness. Belmont watched his surroundings, on edge because he knew nothing of the existing situation around town. Anything could have happened in the short time he had been away. They approached the law office, and Hogben gave no trouble. He walked to the door of the office, thrust it open, and stalked inside, with Belmont following closely. Hogben paused in front of the desk, and Belmont, expecting to see Roscoe Dayne seated there, was faintly surprised to see Sheriff Grant at the desk. The county lawman looked up, plainly irritated by Hogben's presence.

'What in hell do you want, Muley?' Grant demanded. 'I thought I told you I didn't want to see your ugly face until you're due in court.'

'Tell that to the Ranger,' Hogben rasped, and moved aside so the sheriff could see Belmont.

'So you're back,' Grant acknowledged. 'When I got back I found the jail too full of prisoners so I released them until dates have been set for their trials, whatever their charges.'

'When I put someone in jail I expect him to stay there until I say what should happen to him,' Belmont retorted. 'Where is the deputy? I told Dayne to keep all my prisoners behind bars until I returned.'

'I fired Dayne when I returned.' The sheriff was unconcerned by Belmont's manner. 'He's supposed to obey my orders to the letter but he didn't do that so he's out of a job. As for Hogben, he'll be around to answer any charges against him.'

'I need to question him now,' Belmont rapped, 'so he'll go back behind bars until I can get round to him.'

The sheriff opened his mouth to protest, but at that moment Baldy Jex ushered in the two kidnappers, and Grant frowned and stared at the newcomers.

'Who in hell are they, and why are they hogtied?' he demanded.

'These two kidnapped Tilda when. she left the Bar C earlier,' Baldy replied. He gave a terse account of what had happened, and Belmont, listening and watching the sheriff, told himself again that there was something about Grant which he did not like.

'What have you two got to say for yourselves?' Grant asked when Baldy lapsed into silence. 'Do you deny kidnapping?'

'They can't deny it with three witnesses against them,' Baldy said sharply.

'So I'll lock them up,' Grant retorted. 'What do you want to do about Hogben?' He looked at Belmont and awaited his reply.

'Jail him,' Belmont said. 'I need him where I can get to him without having to chase him around the county. Who else have you released from jail? Are Goymer and Stoll still behind bars?'

'Those two are local lawmen.' Grant shook his head. 'I had a talk with Goymer. He reckoned you wasn't wearing your law star when he drew on you, and he figured you as a gunnie causing trouble. Because he was wounded I turned him loose; he'll be on hand when you wanta talk to him.'

'And Stoll?' Belmont asked patiently. 'What excuse did he give you for leading me into a gun trap? And the two men who held me prisoner last night in a shack. They planned to take me out into the desert at dawn and bury me there, and would have done so if Baldy hadn't been watching my back and saved me.'

'I turned Stoll loose. I hate to tell you this, but you've made some bad mistakes, Ranger. You don't know the men around here like I do, and I can vouch for Goymer and Stoll. As for the other two, they're still behind bars.'

'Well that's something, huh?' Belmont rasped. He saw that Hogben was grinning at him, and motioned with his gun. 'I want Hogben back behind bars, and right now. Lock him in, Sheriff, and we'll go into this later. And put these two where they'll be safe until I can talk to them. Right now I want to get some grub and rest up. It's been a hard day.'

Sheriff Grant looked as if he wanted to argue some more, but one look at Belmont's face warned him against doing so. He picked up the cell keys and led the way into the cell block. Belmont stayed close to Hogben, and did not relax until the big man was safely locked behind bars. Baldy continued to menace the two kidnappers until the sheriff had turned a key in the lock of their cell door.

Belmont felt as if there was a heavy burden resting on his shoulders as he walked back into the office. Tilda was waiting for him, seated on a chair by the desk, and he smiled wearily when he met her gaze. She looked exhausted, and carried the unmistakable signs of shock in her taut features.

'Have you finished here now?' she asked.

'I hope so,' he replied.

'I don't know what game you're playing, Sheriff,' she said as Grant emerged from the cell block. 'I always thought all lawmen worked together, but what you've been doing against Clay is probably criminal. How can you turn arrested men loose without getting all the details of their arrest?'

'You don't understand the crafts of law work,' Grant replied huffily. 'All I will say about it is that I considered the arrests from the law's point of view and did what I thought was right. Now let it drop. If Goymer and Stoll are wanted at any time, then let me know and I'll have them brought in immediately. I don't expect any trouble on that score.'

Belmont turned to the street door, and it opened as he reached out to grasp the handle. Kane Orton entered the office to confront him. The rancher's face was set in grim lines.

'I'm glad to see you, Ranger,' he said harshly. 'There's been hell to pay on my range. My outfit caught up with a bunch of rustlers this afternoon after you left me to return to town, and a fight broke out. We shot the hell out of those rustlers.'

'That's good news,' Belmont said instantly.

'Yeah. Well, when we got down to check on them rustlers we found they was the Bar C outfit, led by Asa Camford hisself!'

Belmont froze for a moment, shocked by the revelation, but there was an immediate reaction from Baldy Jex. The old ex-Ranger drew his gun swiftly and thrust the muzzle against Orton's belly.

'By God, if you've killed Asa then you'll follow the same trail pronto,' he rapped.

'Camford got away with a handful of his crew,' Orton said. 'And don't give me that old stuff about him not being guilty because he once rode with the Rangers. I got him dead to rights. Him and his boys were driving a big herd of my cows off my range. We caught 'em in the act. And they started the shooting soon as they saw us. Anything that happened after that was done in self-defence by my outfit.'

'You're a lying rattlesnake!' Tilda said furiously. 'My father is one of the straightest men alive.'

'If that's a fact then why isn't he here giving his side of the business?' Orton's voice was matter of fact. 'I'll tell you why he ain't: the last I saw him he was hightailing it back to Bar C with half my outfit chasing him, and when they catch him he'll be lucky if they don't string him up to the nearest tree.'

'I've warned you before against taking the law into your own hands, Orton,' Herb Grant said fiercely. 'Why didn't you ride in here asking for the law's help? There's a proper way of doing things, and you'll only make trouble for yourself by going off half-cocked.'

'The law in this county is useless,' Orton rapped. 'We've been suffering losses for a long time now, and we ain't gonna stand for it any longer. We declared war on rustlers, and now we've started on them we won't stop until they're all finished.'

'I'm heading back to Bar C pronto,' Baldy Jex said fiercely, 'and if I find you're lying about what happened then I'll come looking for you, Orton. If you've shot down Bar C riders you'll pay for it.' He holstered his gun with a swift movement and stepped around Orton to open the door. 'Come on, Tilda, we're riding out now. There'll be hell to pay if Asa has been hurt.'

The girl ran to the door, such was her haste to get home, and Belmont stood considering his next action as the door slammed. Orton's face was expressionless, but there was an unholy light in his narrowed eyes. Belmont exhaled slowly, his thoughts busy. It looked as if he had reached the point where he would really have to start earning his wages.

Eight

'Tell me in detail what happened on your range, Orton,' Herb Grant said harshly. 'I can't believe a staunch law-and-order man like Asa Camford would do what you said. You must've made a big mistake. Mebbe, in the heat of the moment, you got it wrong.'

'There was no way I mistook it,' Orton spoke furiously. 'Now we know why the law couldn't get a line on the rustlers. Everybody thought it was a gang doing the stealing, but it's plain now that Camford has been running the steal.'

Belmont went to the street door and departed. Closing the door at his back, he walked along the darkened street with long strides. He needed to talk with Asa Camford before he attempted to do anything else, and hurried to the stable, reaching it just as Baldy and Tilda emerged with their mounts.

'Give me a coupla minutes,' he said firmly. 'I wanta ride with you.'

'I was hoping you would,' Baldy replied. as Belmont hurried into the barn.

Belmont saddled up and led his horse outside. He mounted and sided the girl and the old ex-Ranger and they set off along the street at a canter. Passing the law office, Belmont saw that the street door was

open and two figures were standing in the bright
lamplight issuing through it. One was the sheriff,
Belmont noted, and when Grant's voice called out to
him he ignored it and continued. Baldy Jex was
already setting a fast pace, and they soon left Broken
Ridge behind and hit the open trail to the Bar C,
filled with shock and a sense of unreality at Orton's
grim news.

They rode in silence. Tilda was worried about her
father and Baldy seemed filled with foreboding. The
night was dark, but there was enough light from
starshine to give them limited vision. The horses
were tired, but they seemed to sense the uneasiness
gripping their riders and maintained a good pace
over the dark miles of the range.

It was past midnight when Baldy broke the silence.
'We're getting close now.' He spoke in a rasping
tone which betrayed his concern. 'There ain't no
lights showing on the ranch, so slow down and go in
careful. If the outfit ran into trouble today they'll be
on watch with itchy trigger fingers. Let me pull ahead
of you by a few yards.'

As he finished speaking there was an outbreak of
rapid shooting somewhere just ahead, and Belmont
saw gun flashes tattering the screen of darkness. He
had no idea exactly where they were, and reined in
to take stock.

'Take care of Tilda, Clay,' Baldy rapped, and
spurred his horse forward into the shadows.

He was swallowed instantly by the night. Belmont
reached out and grasped the reins of the girl's horse
as she tried to follow the old ex-Ranger, whose reced-
ing hoofbeats quickly faded away to nothing.

'No sense riding into trouble,' Belmont said, as
Tilda tried vainly to pull her reins free of his grasp.

The shooting cut off as suddenly as it had begun, and the ensuing darkness seemed more impenetrable than before.

Belmont strained his ears but heard nothing beyond the sighing breeze. He blinked, fighting off tiredness, but his alertness could not be faulted as he leaned towards the girl's figure.

'How far are we from Bar C?' he asked. 'And exactly where is it from here?'

'We're on the slope of a ridge which is just above us,' she replied. 'The ranch is half a mile on the other side of the ridge, almost due north from here.'

'That shooting was directed at the ranch,' he mused. 'Can you lead me in a half-circle to try and get to the spread from the far side?'

'I'd rather set the horse into a gallop and go straight in, like Baldy,' she responded spiritedly.

'There ain't no sense taking unnecessary risks.' His voice was stern. 'Let's get moving. If we can sneak in then so much the better. No one will know we're on the spot.'

'It must be some of Orton's men doing the shooting,' she said. 'Come on. Angle right and we'll stay in dead ground.'

Belmont followed her as she rode swiftly off to the right, and they entered a gully that soon towered high above them on either hand. Belmont kept his ears strained for more shooting, but they were cut off from everything in the gully, and he had to narrow his eyes to keep Tilda in view.

Presently the ground dropped away again and they emerged from the gully. Tilda reined in immediately, and Belmont nudged his horse close in to her side.

'The ranch is over there to the left,' she said in a

harsh whisper. 'We'd better get down and walk in from here.'

'There could be shooting from some of your crew if they spot us moving,' he warned.

'I don't think they'd open fire without challenging first,' she responded, sliding out of her saddle. She looped her reins around the saddlehorn and patted the animal's rump to send it away. When she began striding off to the left, Belmont hurriedly dismounted, trailed his reins, and followed her, taking long strides in order to catch up with her.

'Who's moving in over there?' a harsh voice challenged from the shadows to the right. 'Hold up there, you two. We got to wait for more help before we can finish this.'

'That's not one of our riders,' Tilda said softly. 'He must be one of the rustlers. They've got the place surrounded.'

Belmont halted when the voice spoke, and gazed in the direction from whence it had come but saw nothing.

'Come over here, you two,' the voice continued. 'Make it quick or I'll start shooting.'

Belmont turned towards Tilda, who was already resuming her move in the direction of the ranch. He placed himself between the girl and the unknown challenger, gritting his teeth as he drew his gun and prepared to fight.

'Wait a minute,' he said in an undertone. 'Get down here and stay put until I come back. I'll go over to that man and try to find out something about the situation.'

'You can't do that,' she protested, turning to him, and he pulled her down to the ground in case shooting started. 'They'll gun you down on sight.'

'Two can play at that game,' he retorted. 'Wait here until I come back.'

He arose, not giving her time to argue, and walked in the direction the voice had sounded.

'Make it quick,' the man called again. 'What in hell are you doin'? You were told to surround the house and stay quiet until more help arrived.'

Belmont was straining his eyes to get a glimpse of the speaker, and suddenly saw a faint movement in the darkness. He spotted a man's figure, and saw that he was covered by a six-gun. He was holding his own weapon, and levelled it at the man.

'Who are you?' the man demanded again. 'We got so many new men on the payroll I don't know half of you. What in hell was you thinking about, moving in on your own? Don't you know we got to do this right? Bar C is a tough outfit.'

Belmont reached the man's side and, covered by the darkness, struck out with the barrel of his Colt, at the same time sidestepping the man's levelled weapon. His blow caught the man's gunhand, and there was a gasp of pain as the weapon thudded on the ground. Belmont stepped in half a pace and threw his left fist in a powerful hook. His knuckles smacked solidly against the man's jaw and he reached out and caught the body as it crumpled to the ground.

He grasped the man, swung him up across his left shoulder, and started back to where he had left Tilda, but another voice yelled at him.

'Hey you! Hold it right there. What's going on?'

Belmont turned with the prisoner still across his shoulder, and levelled his gun as a figure appeared from the gloom.

'What's this about?' the man demanded, halting just out of arm's length. 'Who's that you're carrying?'

Belmont cocked his gun and the other moved back in alarm.

'No gunplay,' he snapped. 'We've got to keep it quiet.'

Belmont squeezed off a shot, aiming for the man's right shoulder. He was in a tight spot and knew it could only get worse if he hesitated. He blinked against the gun flash. The man spun away into the darkness. Shouts sounded hard on the echoes of the shot, and Belmont dumped his burden and ran back to where he had left Tilda. He needed to get a slant on the situation, and dearly wanted a prisoner. But his luck was out and he was feeling desperate as he retreated, being unable to get to grips with the facts of the crooked business.

Tilda was waiting, and Belmont grasped her arm and pulled her upright. At that moment several guns started shooting from behind, and he pushed her down again and joined her as a bullet crackled past his left ear.

'I hoped to take a prisoner we could question,' he told her when the shooting broke off. 'Come on, let's get you into the house.'

They crawled forward several yards before getting to their feet and running. A sudden burst of shooting on the far side of the ranch startled them, and Belmont moved faster to get level with the girl.

'Get down in cover,' he said, grasping her arm. 'There won't be any challenges from your outfit while lead is flying.'

'We're nearly there now,' she responded, jerking herself free of his grasp. 'Just keep your head down and run as fast as you can.' She started running again, and Belmont cursed under his breath and followed her blindly.

A gun crashed from somewhere ahead, its flash staining the darkness, and he heard a slug whine over his head. It had been fired deliberately high, he realized, and then heard a voice challenging them.

'It's Tilda and the Ranger,' the girl replied shrilly, her voice cutting through the fading echoes of the shooting. 'Hold your fire. Cover our backs. There are rustlers behind us.'

Belmont was not happy with the situation. He heard a gun fire from somewhere behind them and a bullet plunked into the ground only inches away from him. He hastened forward, trying to gain on the girl, and then saw the black pile of a building just ahead and followed Tilda forward to it and in through an open doorway.

Two figures materialized from the blackness, and Belmont caught the glint of starshine on naked gunmetal.

'You should know better than this, Tilda,' a harsh voice said. 'It's dangerous on the range at the moment. Why in hell are you running around in the open? We heard, when we got back here, that you'd left on your own to look for the boss.'

'Is my father all right?' she demanded.

'He took a slug through his leg but it ain't serious. We lost some men though. We rode into an ambush.'

'Who set the ambush, do you know?' Belmont cut in.

'Who's this, Tilda?' Suspicion filled the questioning tone.

This is Clay Belmont, a Texas Ranger,' Tilda replied.

'Glory be!' came the immediate reply. 'Has he come here to help us or arrest us?'

'Why should I want to arrest you?' Belmont asked. 'Have you broken the law?'

'No, but we figure the men who ambushed us have got the county law in their pocket, and no doubt Herb Grant is being told a tale that will blame us for what's happened today. There's gonna be hell to pay right through the county now.'

'We were in the sheriff's office when Kane Orton showed up with the news that he and his outfit caught the Bar C crew rustling one of his herds,' Belmont said firmly. 'He said it turned to shooting, and Bar C is to blame.'

'Kane Orton!' repeated the Bar C man. 'I never saw him at the ambush. And it didn't happen like he said. We caught up with a crooked bunch who were rustling KO steers and pitched into them when they started shooting at us. But they wasn't KO riders. They was all strangers. We hadn't set eyes on any of them before.'

'Where is my father?' Tilda cut in.

'Lying on the couch in his office. He ain't gonna be able to get around much for a coupla weeks.'

'Did Baldy come in through the yard?' Belmont asked.

'He sure did. That old fire-eater puts us all to shame. He's up front now, wanting to sashay out and hit those ambushers before they know what's happening.'

'Come with me, Clay,' Tilda said urgently. 'You've been wanting to meet my pa.'

Belmont followed her. It was dark inside the house and she clasped his hand and led him. He walked into a half-open door and smothered a curse.

'Not so fast,' he warned. I'm a stranger here and I can't see in the dark.'

Dim light gleamed suddenly, and they entered a room which was illuminated by a lamp. Heavy curtains were drawn across a window, and Belmont looked around quickly at the several men present. He saw Baldy Jex crouching beside a man sprawled out on a low couch, and the ex-Ranger got to his feet when he saw Belmont.

'Glad you made it, Clay,' he said. 'I'm trying to get Asa to let me take some men out there and carry the fight to that crooked bunch. No sense waiting for their reinforcements.'

'I almost had me a prisoner,' Belmont replied. 'Just bad luck my bluff didn't work.'

'This here is Asa Camford,' Baldy introduced. 'Him and me and your pa rode through Texas as Rangers before you was born, son.'

'I'm pleased to meet you, Clay.' Camford looked his age at the moment. He had been a big man in his prime, but a lot of his flesh had wasted away and he looked like someone just getting over a long illness. The left leg of his pants had been slit open to above the knee and a bloodstained bandage was wrapped around his thin leg. But there was a six-gun lying near to his right hand, and he looked like a man who would not turn away from a fight.

'I've heard a lot about you, Asa,' Belmont replied. 'I'm sure sorry to see you like this. I wish I had got into the county earlier. I would have been, too, but I had a job to do below the Border before I could come on here. Now it looks like I got a real bad mess to clean up.'

'From what I've been hearing, you didn't waste any time when you did arrive,' Camford replied. 'Thanks for saving Tilda back there in town. I'll take the matter up with the men concerned soon as we've beaten this rustling problem.'

'I've been wanting to meet you for a talk,' Belmont said. He paused when a spate of shooting sent a string of echoes hammering through the night. 'But I guess that can wait until we've sorted out this business. Tell me what happened to you today.'

'I took my crew out when I learned that a bunch of my cows had been lifted off our south range,' Camford said tiredly.

'Your south range adjoins Kane Orton's north range, huh?' Belmont asked.

'That's right. We made a wide sweep, and picked up tracks, but lost them eventually in hard ground to the south-west. On the way back I figured to check Orton's north pastures to see if he'd been hit like us, and we ran into mebbe a dozen hardcases hazing along a big herd of Orton's beef. We started shooting but there were too many for us, although that crooked bunch finally lit out leaving Orton's cows standing. We took out after them but they got away, and when I decided to call it a day those jaspers came back and hit us again. They sure were tricky and we lost some men. They chased us all the way back here, and from what Baldy says, they've surrounded the place and mean to put us under. But I guess they ain't got enough guns now. They been holding off for more than two hours.'

'They're waiting for more men to come up,' Belmont said. 'I grabbed one of them on the way in but had to let him go. He said something about dumping the blame for the rustling on you. Kane Orton came into the sheriff's office while we were there and said his outfit had caught Bar C taking his cows.'

'That's a lie!' Camford shook his head. 'None of us saw any of the KO outfit on the other side. The crooked bunch we tangled with was all strangers to us.'

'How would Orton know about the shooting if he wasn't there?' Belmont asked.

'There's only one way to find out what is going on,' Baldy said impatiently. 'We got to take a couple of prisoners and make 'em talk. If you're planning on going out there, Clay, then I'm the man to side you.'

Belmont shook his head. 'Sorry, Baldy. It's a one-man job. If you came along and we got separated we could easily end up shooting at each other. You stick around here and keep Bar C on its toes. Just don't shoot me when I come back in.'

'Heck, I shoulda gone out there before you showed up,' Baldy complained, shaking his head.

'If you've got any thoughts on who might be at the back of the rustling then tell me before I leave,' Belmont said. 'I was told that Muley Hogben is handling some of the rustling, which could tie in Orton's bunch, but I need proof before I can do anything.'

'How did you hear about Hogben?' Baldy asked. 'And if he is involved then don't forget who his friends are around town.'

'Sim Goymer for one.' Belmont nodded. 'I'll get round to him in time, and the rest of those men we picked up in town.' He drew his six-gun and checked its loads. 'I'm concerned about the kidnapping attempts on Tilda.' He glanced at the girl, who was standing silently by her father's side. 'I take it you won't try to leave the ranch again, huh?'

'Not now my father is here,' she replied. 'If we are attacked by the rustlers I'll be at one of the windows like the rest of the men. I can handle a rifle as well as any of them.'

'Don't shoot me,' Belmont smiled grimly. 'Make sure none of your men are moving around outside while I'm gone. We don't want accidents occurring. And warn everyone that I'm out there moving around.'

'I'd feel happier if I went with you,' Baldy said.

'Forget it.' Belmont shook his head. 'Someone's got to organize a defence in here. The rustlers are waiting for reinforcements, and there's no telling when they'll show up. That's why I wanta get moving. See me out, Baldy, and then seal off the place. There are a lot of men moving around out there.'

'This way,' Baldy said, and led Belmont to the rear of the house, pausing inside the kitchen. 'Come in this way when you're ready, Clay. I'll warn the men in here to expect you.'

Belmont nodded and slipped outside when Baldy opened the door for him. He moved silently out of the sanctuary of the house and walked slowly into the darkness, gun in hand, his nerves hair-triggered. He was surprised to make an uneventful crossing to the side of a barn, and paused in its shelter, hugging the deep shadows as he looked around and listened for signs of the rustlers.

The breeze filled his ears and he squatted and slitted his eyes, looking for movement and listening intently for tell-tale sound. A horse stamped somewhere beyond the barn and he turned instantly, moving to the rear of the building. When he reached the rear corner and walked boldly around it the muzzle of a rifle jabbed him in the stomach and a harsh voice warned him to remain still.

'Who are you?' a man growled. 'What in hell are you moving around for?'

'I got orders for you,' Belmont said unhesitatingly, taking a fresh grip on his drawn six-gun. He felt the pressure of the rifle muzzle ease away from his stomach and slid his left foot forward half a pace as his left fist swung in a tight arc for the unknown man's jaw. His knuckles landed with a satisfying crunch and he struck with his six-gun, knocking the menacing rifle barrel to one side.

The weapon exploded with a flat crack, and Belmont lifted his gun and struck for the head. The man fell in a sprawling heap and lay still. Belmont breathed deeply as he took weapons from the man and threw them away into the gloom. This was not going according to plan.

He straightened, gun in hand, and pressed his back against the rear wall of the barn. Now he could hear a number of horses moving uneasily and snuffling, and went forward along the back of the barn until he reached a line of six horses tied to a rope stretched out as a picket line between two convenient trees.

So there were at least six men around the ranch, he thought, and began untying the horses. When they were all free he pointed the muzzle of his six-gun skywards and fired a couple of shots, sending the horses fleeing madly for other parts. He grinned tensely when the sound of their hooves faded away in the darkness. They could not be rounded up before daybreak.

He waited beside the other rear corner of the barn, which overlooked the yard and corrals, and stood watching the shadows. Presently a dark figure appeared from across the yard and came slowly towards the barn. He stood motionless and silent, and when the man came within arm's length he struck with the speed and silence of a preying rattlesnake.

Grasping the man's gunhand by closing his fingers around the man's wrist, he swung his Colt and hit the man with the barrel, aiming for the back of the head just below the hatbrim. The man went down silently, and Belmont disarmed him swiftly.

He went back along the rear of the barn and moved in a wide circle around the house, looking for more rustlers, wanting to disarm all those present before reinforcements arrived, but, as he left the cover of the barn, he heard the ominous sound of many hooves out there in the night, galloping relentlessly towards the ranch.

Changing his plan, he went back to the nearest of the men he had rendered harmless, hoisted him across his left shoulder, and went unerringly back to the kitchen door of the house, walking openly, aware that Baldy would have arranged with his men to admit him without trouble.

A guarded voice called urgently to him when he was within ten yards, and he gave his name as he covered the remaining distance. The sound of approaching horses was much louder and clearer, and when he reached the open door of the kitchen Baldy Jex appeared in the doorway.

'Take the prisoner,' Belmont said, and eager hands relieved him of the unconscious man. 'I'm not coming in. There's a big bunch of riders coming in and I wanta find out their plans. Keep the place covered, Baldy, and be ready to fight.'

'We're ready,' Baldy retorted. 'Be careful out there.'

Belmont faded away into the shadows, silent, dangerous like a lobo wolf. He went swiftly towards the sound of approaching hooves, ready for action.

Nine

Belmont reached the edge of the yard by the side of the house and saw at least a dozen riders arriving from the open range. They turned into the corral and dismounted, some talking vociferously, and there was some harsh laughter as they trailed their reins and gathered in a group. Belmont saw the glint of faint moonlight on drawn weapons, and a sense of remoteness filled him when he realized that these men had no compunction about what they were planning to do.

They had come to fight the Bar C outfit. They were gathering like any hunting party, but they were not after game. They were here to kill honest men in the futherance of their crimes, and Belmont breathed shallowly as he checked his six-gun and readied himself for action.

'Spread out, you men.' someone ordered in a firm voice. 'Surround the place and, when you start shooting, aim to kill. Nobody on the ranch is to remain alive. Orton has given the word. Now get to it.'

Belmont's eyes glinted at the name. Orton! There it was again. And he recalled that the two men in Broken Ridge who had been waiting to kidnap Tilda Camford had mentioned the same name. He had confounded those men at that time, and now he meant to do it again, here and now.

He watched the men moving away from the corral, and it was in him to start shooting. But that was not the way he worked. He was a lawman, and although he knew exactly what this gang proposed to do he could not open the action. He would wait until they involved themselves by shooting before attempting to deal with them.

Easing back around the front corner of the house he leaned against the wall of the building and allowed the tense moments to flit by. His eyes were accustomed to the shadows, and he saw figures out there casually taking up positions and checking their weapons.

Finally a single shot blasted out through the heavy silence of the night and a bullet thudded into the front of the house.

'Go to it, men!' a raucous voice yelled, and its echoes were drowned in a volley of shots that hammered painfully against Belmont's eardrums.

Dropping to one knee, Belmont cocked his six-gun and narrowed his eyes. A window in the front of the house, only a yard or so to his left, began to emit gun flashes, and shooting erupted, sporadically at first, then with growing volume. He peered around the corner and saw half-a-dozen figures running in towards the porch from across the yard, and now guns were firing steadily from all the front windows.

Belmont lifted his Colt and aimed at the nearest figure, but it fell to the ground before he could fire and he swung his muzzle and drew a bead on another. Squeezing his trigger, he saw the figure pitch sideways as if it had been swatted by a giant hand. The next instant he was firing rapidly, and the attackers quickly realized that resistance from the house was too strong for them. The attack faltered and then halted in the dust of the yard. Three survivors turned to run back to safety, and Belmont cut down one of them before they had covered three yards. The other two also fell before reaching cover.

The shooting ceased then and an uneasy silence settled over the ranch as the grim echoes faded. Belmont fed fresh shells into his smoking Colt, breathing shallowly through clenched teeth as he did so. Gunsmoke was acrid in his nostrils. No one was moving now around the yard, and he wondered what orders Orton had given for such an eventuality. The rustlers had evidently felt that they could easily over-come any resistance.

Watching his surroundings intently while his thoughts roved, Belmont became aware of a faint glow of fire beyond the corral which was moving slowly, circling the corral, and he realized that the attackers had piled straw into a wagon, ignited it, and were pushing the wagon towards the house. He clenched his teeth and lifted his gun, waiting until he could see targets clearly.

A bunch of men were grouped behind the wagon, which shielded them from Bar C guns covering the front of the house, and it continued to roll forward despite the shooting directed at it. But Belmont had the advantage of being at a slight angle and could clearly see the men behind the vehicle. He dropped to one knee and began to shoot, triggering his gun rapidly, aiming for legs. His shots had an immediate effect. The attack died quickly, with surviving men running back to the corral, and four men were left lying in the yard, writhing and squirming with leg wounds. The wagon remained in the centre of the

yard, burning fiercely, spreading light over the front
of the house and illuminating the yard perfectly for
the defenders.

Belmont reloaded as he moved back along the
side of the house, not forgetting to duck below a
window which was covered by the defenders. He
reached the rear corner of the building just as men
came from the barn to attack the kitchen doorway,
and opened fire, aiming his shots and streaking the
shadows with reddish flame as his deadly gun did its
grim work.

Bullets began to slam into the woodwork around
him, and he saw gun flashes in the deep gloom
around the barn. Then a slug punched through the
crown of his Stetson and he dropped flat and rolled
to a new position. The fight was hotting up. He could
only wonder how many rustlers were present and why
they were so determined to kill off the Bar C outfit.

The shooting ceased as if a tacit agreement existed
between attackers and defenders. An uneasy silence
settled. Gunsmoke blew into Belmont's face and he
wrinkled his nose. Getting to his feet, he reloaded his
gun and stood waiting and watching, deadly six-gun
in hand. He could hear voices coming across the
distance separating him from the barn, and most of
them were protesting about the heavy resistance they
were facing. He was tempted to get to close quarters
and carry the fight to the attackers, but decided that
the time was not right for such audacity.

It was well that he stayed his hand for the next
instant another attack came in. Belmont compressed
his lips and narrowed his eyes as he started shooting.
Gun flashes tattered the darkness as dark figures
came running quickly towards the house. Belmont
dropped to one knee and fired rapidly, and two guns

were also firing from the kitchen doorway to his right.

The rustlers faded away, those unhurt dropping to the ground and squirming away into the comparative safety of the shadows. Belmont reloaded again, taking fresh shells from the loops in his cartridge belt, certain now that the attackers had taken more than their fill of hot lead. As tense minutes passed it seemed that the shooting was over, and a few moments later he heard the sound of departing horses from the corral. He listened until the sounds had faded away to nothing, then approached the back door.

'Hello there! This is Clay Belmont, the Texas Ranger. I'm coming in.'

'Come right ahead, Clay,' Baldy Jex answered, and emerged from the house as Belmont walked towards him. 'Say that was a humdinger while it lasted, huh? Have they pulled out for good, do you think?'

'Perhaps they haven't all gone,' Belmont responded.

'Yeah, well, there are a lot of them who'll never leave.' Baldy chuckled. 'We sure fed 'em lead in lethal doses.'

'Don't relax here in the house.' Belmont paused and looked around, peering into the shadows, watching for furtive movement. 'I'll take a look around and see what's doing. Don't let anyone do any more shooting unless you're fired on from out there. I want to be able to come and go without risking a bullet.'

'Want me to go along with you?' Baldy asked. 'I could cover you.'

'I'd rather have you here in control,' Belmont replied. 'I'll sing out when I want to come back in.'

'You got it.' Baldy slapped Belmont's broad shoulder and went back into the shelter of the house.

Belmont walked out into the open, making for the barn, and paused to check the men he found lying in the shadows. There were five between the rear of the house and the barn, all dead, mute testament to the skill of the defenders. When he reached the barn he paused in dense shadow and listened intently for noise, and heard nothing but the sighing of the breeze and other natural night noises.

He went around the back of the barn and approached the corral, moving slowly, silently. When he was able to see the yard, still faintly illuminated by the dying fire of the burning wagon, he shook his head at the sight of at least a dozen silent figures lying motionless where they had fallen haphazardly. There was no movement anywhere, and he figured that the rest of the rustlers had pulled out.

When he heard the sudden clatter of hooves off to his right he went swiftly in that direction and came upon a man trying to drag himself into the saddle of a nervously cavorting horse.

'Stand still, yuh dumb bronc!' a harsh voice rasped.

Belmont went forward with ready gun. 'Stand still,' he snapped. 'Get your hands up. You're not going anywhere, mister.'

He was ready for the quick movement of the man's reaction to his harsh command, and stepped in close, aware of a weapon in the man's hand. He reached for and grasped the man's right wrist, twisting the hand upwards. The six-gun blasted, dazzling his eyes with its brilliant flash, but the bullet whined away into the night sky and Belmont struck with the barrel of his Colt, slamming the hard metal against the man's head.

The man crumpled, and Belmont went down with him, still gripping the hand holding the gun. He lifted his weapon to strike again but another blow was unnecessary and he dragged the Colt from the unconscious man's hand.

Looking around, Belmont ensured that he was not being stalked, and wiped sweat from his forehead. He squatted by his prisoner until the man regained consciousness, then dragged him upright and thrust him against the poles of the corral with such force that the breath was knocked out of his lungs. He grasped a handful of the man's shirt with his left hand and held him steady while he thrust the muzzle of his gun under the man's nose.

'Hold it,' the man said weakly. 'I know when I've had enough. It's over for me. I got a bullet in my side and I'm losing blood fast. We didn't expect a tough fight. Who you got here, cavalry?'

'It's over for the whole bunch of you,' Belmont said grimly. 'You're under arrest, mister. I'm a Texas Ranger. Tell me who you are and what is going on here and I'll see that you get some help for your wound.'

'I got nothing to say.' The man stifled a groan. 'My life wouldn't be worth a plugged nickel if I talked. The gang is a real tough outfit.'

'They didn't seem so tough when they walked into our fire, and they've just pulled out.'

'They'll be back by dawn.' The man spoke in a matter-of-fact tone. 'They can't let this rest here. They'll bring more men and finish you.'

'Let's get over to the house.' Belmont grasped the

man's shoulder and dragged him away from the corral. 'If we meet any of your pards on the way you better identify yourself to them and stop them shooting. If you don't, I'll send you to Hell myself. You got that?'

'Yeah. I'm out of this now.' The man sagged against Belmont, who used considerable strength to hold him upright.

Belmont half-carried the man towards the house, skirting the yard and making for the kitchen door. Baldy Jex stepped out into the open in response to Belmont's guarded call and helped get the prisoner inside the building. Baldy was almost buzzing with excitement.

'Someone ain't shooting as well as he should,' he observed. 'And I told everyone to shoot to kill. But we can soon send this galoot on his way. We'll string him up in the barn before breakfast. He won't be the first rustler we've nudged into Hell.'

'You're the law, ain't you?' the prisoner demanded. 'You can't let them hang me.'

'Answer the questions I got and you won't have anything to worry about.' Belmont replied. 'You'd be a key witness and I'd take good care of you. Who's running the rustlers?'

'I'm bleeding bad,' the man gasped, sagging against Baldy, who was supporting him.

'Answer the questions and I'll take care of you,' the old ex-Ranger rasped. 'Where'd you stop the slug?'

The man fell sideways and Belmont reached out and grasped him. They carried him through the kitchen and into the lighted room where Asa Camford was lying. Tilda was sitting by her father's side, seemingly frozen in shock. Baldy checked the rustler, and shook his head when he looked up at Belmont.

'He's been hit mighty bad, Clay,' he said. 'You'll be lucky to get anything out of him.'

'Give him a swig of something strong,' Belmont said. 'And your outfit better remain alert. He said something about the rustlers coming back at dawn. They've pulled out to get more help.'

Baldy fetched a bottle of whiskey and poured some of its contents into the man's mouth. Belmont could see a patch of blood on the man's left side just above the waist. The rustler's face was ashen in the lamp-light. He was semi-conscious and looked far gone. There were beads of sweat on his forehead.

'Can you hear me?' Belmont spoke harshly. 'Tell me about the rustling. Who's back of it?'

The prisoner's eyes flickered open. 'You'll find that out soon enough,' he said with an effort. 'The rest of the gang will be back. Orton said he'd fetch the KO outfit. They'll be here around dawn. That's all I can tell you.'

'You're saying that the KO ain't behind the stealing?' Belmont queried. 'If that gun crew wasn't Orton's KO outfit then what bunch of men has Orton been using?'

'Professional rustlers. They came from all over the south-west. The plan is for the biggest cattle steal ever.'

'Seems to me we shot the backbone out of that gang,' Baldy commented as he checked the man's wound. He looked up at Belmont and shook his head slightly. 'It don't matter who's running the shebang. If the rest of the bunch show up here at dawn we'll give 'em hell.'

A cowboy came to the door of the room and

peered inside. 'Baldy,' he said urgently, 'we can hear at least a dozen horses moving in fast from the trail. Sounds like the gunnies are coming back. Wanta check it out?'

Belmont and Baldy went to the front of the house.

'When I got in I sent word to Frank Weston of the Flying W to bring his outfit here,' Baldy said. 'They're close neighbours and have had a lot of trouble with rustlers. With any luck it'll be Frank coming in now. If it is then we can plan a hot reception for the rustlers if they do come back at dawn.'

'That was good thinking, Baldy,' Belmont said.

'Once a Ranger always a Ranger,' Baldy responded.

They reached the front door and eased out to the porch. The burning wagon was now barely illuminating the surrounding area but Belmont caught a glimpse of movement out by the corral.

'Hello, the house,' a voice yelled. 'This is Frank Weston. What's been going on here? Looks like you had some trouble.'

'Frank, put your horses in the corral and get your men over here pronto,' Baldy yelled. 'We're expecting the rustlers back at dawn.'

Belmont watched carefully as men came forward across the yard.

'It's the Flying W outfit,' Baldy assured him. 'Now we can make plans to finish the rustlers.'

Frank Weston was a short, fleshy, powerfully built man who waddled across the yard and breezed into the house. He wore a sagging gunbelt around his huge waist and carried a rifle.

'What in hell has been going on here, Baldy?' he boomed wheezily, his big chest rising and falling. 'Those dead men out there. Are they rustlers?'

'We figure they are, Frank,' Baldy replied. 'They were around the place when I got back from Broken Ridge, and they've sure been attacking us. Looked like they meant to finish us off. But we swatted them some and they hightailed it.'

'You should have sent for us earlier,' Weston said. 'I've been wanting to have a crack at those pesky rustlers. Are you sure they're coming back?'

'We're hoping they will,' Baldy said.

'Well, we're here now.' Weston looked at Belmont and observed the Ranger badge on his shirt front.

'I heard you'd showed up in Broken Ridge,' he said breezily. 'You sure stamped your foot on the hardcases running the town. Sim Goymer and his kind. They been strangling the county since they got a foot in the door. Pity you didn't kill Goymer while you was at it.'

'His law badge saved him,' Belmont admitted. He counted twelve newcomers as they came across the yard and entered the house. 'It looks like you'll do the business if the rustlers come back, Baldy. You won't need me here, huh?'

'What you planning to do?' Baldy asked.

'I've a mind to ride back to Broken Ridge and start a clean up of my own. I've got a lot of questions to put to certain men back there, and now seems a pretty good time to leave. I'd like to make a start as soon as possible.'

'Heck, you can't ride out alone,' Baldy protested. 'You're gonna need an old ex-Ranger to side you. There are enough guns here now to handle the rustlers, if they come back. I'll ride with you, Clay. You're gonna need someone who's got local knowledge. Heck, the names of several townsmen are coming to mind right now; men who could answer some of the questions you've a mind to ask. You can't ride out alone, Clay, not nohow.'

'Talk to Asa about it while I try to find my horse out there,' Belmont said. 'I had to leave it on the way in. I'll go out the back door.'

Baldy led Frank Weston into Asa Camford's office, and Belmont heard the Flying W boss booming a greeting to the Bar C rancher. Going to the kitchen door, Belmont had hardly stepped outside when Baldy was at his side, grasping his arm.

'Asa agrees with me,' he said. 'You need my help.'

'So let's go,' Belmont said grimly. He whistled shrilly through his teeth and almost immediately there was an answering whinny from his horse.

'Say, that's a good trick,' Baldy observed. 'You got that hoss trained like a dog, Clay. Give me a few minutes to find some hossflesh and we'll split the breeze for town.'

'I'll be at the corral,' Belmont replied. 'I need to use another horse, Baldy. Mine had a hard time of it yesterday.'

'We got plenty of horses,' Baldy said eagerly. 'Let's get moving, Clay. I'll get a lot of satisfaction from riding into Broken Ridge with you. Some men there need taking down a peg or two.'

Belmont nodded. The sheriff, for one, had a lot of explaining to do, and now was the time for questions to be asked.

They were ready to hit the trail within a few minutes, and Belmont, mounted on a fresh horse and eager to be on his way, gave Baldy the signal to get moving. They left the Bar C nestling in its cover of darkness and awaiting the return of the rustlers, and headed fast along the trail that led to Broken Ridge. It was showdown time, and Belmont could only hope he had the measure of those lawless men who had been holding the whole county to ransom. . . .

Ten

Dawn was beginning to claw lighter streaks in the even blackness of the sky when Belmont and Baldy sighted Broken Ridge lying silent and still after a peaceful night. Belmont eased himself tiredly in his saddle. He had been drowsing for most of the trip, and knew Baldy must be exhausted, but the oldster was hunched stolidly in his creaking saddle, grimly anticipating the coming showdown.

'I figure we can get ourselves some coffee and a bite to eat before we start doing the law's work,' Baldy observed. 'What do you say, Clay?'

'You get all the right ideas at the right time,' Belmont responded. 'I sure feel hung over right now, but a bite to eat will set me up for what's to be done.'

'Come on then.' Baldy urged his mount forward and they descended a long slope that led to the town's outer limits. No lights were showing anywhere, and Broken Ridge looked like a ghost town in the early morning.

Belmont moistened his dry lips as he envisaged breakfast. He could almost smell bacon, eggs and coffee, and wondered where Baldy could get food at this early hour.

Baldy circled the outskirts of the town and they

rode in behind a building where lamplight showed in a small window.

'This is the back of Dan's eating-house,' Baldy said as they dismounted and trailed their reins. 'Best food in town is cooked here. We gotta eat before we start hunting skunks. I'm wondering what's going on at Bar C now. With Frank Weston's outfit on the ranch, I kinda feel sorry for those rustlers should they show up.'

'I wish I could be in two places at once,' Belmont mused.

He followed Baldy to the back door of the eating-house, and they entered a kitchen where a man and a woman were busy cooking at the big stove. The man, tall and thin and wearing a grubby white apron, looked up and grinned at the sight of the ex-Ranger.

'Heck, you're astir early this morning, Baldy,' he commented. 'Want the usual?'

'Sure thing. This is Clay Belmont, Texas Ranger, Dan. Feed us well, huh? We got some work to do soon as daylight shows.'

'Sit down at the table and I'll fill a couple of plates. We ain't open yet, but the early feeders will be showing up any time now.'

'What's been going on around town since yesterday?' Baldy asked.

'The usual stuff. Herb Grant came back yesterday, and he turned loose half the prisoners in the jail. He took the deputy badge from Roscoe Dayne, but Roscoe hadn't put a foot wrong any place. He even took a slug when some hardcases tried to bust his prisoners loose yesterday morning. There's some bad feeling in town right now. But you know what folks are like around here: nobody dares do anything against the big men.'

Belmont listened to the chat that passed between Baldy and Dan. The woman brought them two mugs of coffee, and the chill departed from Belmont's stomach as he sipped the fiery black liquid. Then, loaded plates of food were placed before them and silence ensued while they ate.

Belmont was feeling a tiny itch in his chest, a build-up of anticipation because action was due to commence. He finished eating, pushed back his chair and drew his six-gun to check it. Baldy nodded slowly, his eyes narrowing as he watched.

'What's the first move, Clay,' the oldster demanded. 'I'm here to back you up to the hilt. But I'd like to know what's on your mind. I'm wondering if your first move will be what I would have done a few years ago.'

'I'm not happy with the way the sheriff is handling his duties,' Belmont replied without hesitation, 'so I figure to check out the jail first off, and if Grant has turned any more of my prisoners loose then he's gonna see the inside of his own cells. I need a firm base to work from, and the jail is the best spot.'

'I'd throw Grant in a cell without checking him out,' Baldy said. 'He's never done more than he had to to get by, and the fact that we've got so much rustler trouble in the county is on account of he's never done his job properly. You could do worse than fetch in Roscoe Dayne. He'll keep your prisoners behind bars, and he's the only lawman around here who can be trusted.'

'If you're ready then we'll visit the jail,' Belmont decided.

Baldy got to his feet and they left the eating-house. Sunlight was beginning to bathe the range, and Belmont looked around the rutted street as his range of vision increased. There were some men on the sidewalks now, and a few were beginning to converge on the eating-house.

'There's something I don't understand,' Baldy said. 'I can't believe Kane Orton could have got to town when he did if he had witnessed Bar C stealing his herd on his northern line. It would mean him being in two places at once. We rode back into town from his line shack and he showed up here just afterwards. From what Asa told me of the location where his outfit ran into that bunch of rustlers, I'd say Orton, if he'd been there, would have taken another two hours at least to get to town.'

Belmont nodded as they crossed the wide street and walked towards the jail. 'I've been thinking about that myself,' he said. 'Bar C said they didn't recognize any of the rustlers during the shooting. So where was the KO bunch? Orton definitely said it was his outfit that ran Bar C off his northern line.'

'So he was lying,' Baldy said firmly. 'But why he'd do it is another matter, huh?'

'Anyone lying to the law has got to be up to no good,' Belmont observed. 'I got the feeling that today will put an end to a lot of the crooked business around here.'

They reached the law office and Belmont opened the door and entered with Baldy crowding him eagerly. An old man was seated at the desk, a double-barrelled shotgun lying close to hand. The oldster looked up. He was a short man, with grey hair and a haggard face. He reached for the shotgun at the sight of Belmont, then stayed his hand when he saw Baldy.

'Howdy, Dave.' Baldy went to the side of the desk and reached down to place a hand on the shotgun.

'What for you handling guns at your time of life?'

'Howdy, Baldy. Grant asked me to take over the jailer job. He fired Roscoe Dayne yesterday.'

'Yeah. We know. Have you got some prisoners, Dave?' Baldy opened the shotgun and withdrew two cartridges. He put the gun back on the desk. 'Where is Grant now? Do you know, Dave?'

'Heck, he ain't been around since last night! Said he's leaving early this morning to take care of some personal business over Tascos way.'

'He's just got back from handling some personal business,' Belmont frowned. 'When does he find time to enforce the law?'

'He said he's gonna put Roscoe Dayne back into office. Roscoe stopped a slug in the arm yesterday, but he'll be fit for duty. Roscoe will be here some time early this morning, and I'm on duty until he shows.'

'I'd like to take a look at your prisoners,' Belmont said, and the oldster got up from the desk and reached for the big bunch of keys. 'You can stay here,' Belmont continued, taking the keys. 'I want to question some of the men I brought in yesterday.'

'Sure. I don't have anything to do with the prisoners. I'm only here to see they stay behind bars. I wouldn't open one of those occupied cells for anything.'

'Stay here in the office, Baldy,' Belmont said. 'We don't know who might drop in.'

Belmont went to the door in the back wall and unlocked it, passing through and going on to check out the cells. None of his prisoners were behind bars, and, when he saw that Hogben was not present, he shook his head. Turning on his heel, he returned to the office, locking the heavy door at his back.

'All my prisoners have been turned loose,' he told Baldy. 'Where does Grant live when he's not here?'

'At the hotel,' Baldy said. 'You want me to fetch him?'

'We'll go together.' Belmont returned the keys to the desk and made for the door.

They were approaching the hotel when Herb Grant appeared in the doorway of the large building and paused to look around the street. He was smoking a cigar, and looking like a man who was at peace with the world. Then his gaze alighted upon Belmont and Baldy and he stiffened, his expression changing swiftly. He threw away his cigar and took a step towards the sidewalk, then thought better of the action and spun on his heel to re-enter the hotel hurriedly.

Belmont was twenty yards from the hotel and flowed into action as the sheriff disappeared from sight. He ran forward, drawing his gun as he did so, and lunged into the hotel. He blundered across the lobby, spotting Grant making for a door under the big staircase.

'Hold it, Sheriff!' he called. 'I wanta talk to you.'

Grant dragged at the door but it was locked and did not budge. The sheriff turned then, and there was desperation in his taut expression. He dropped a hand to his holstered gun, and Belmont, gun in hand, halted in his tracks and lifted his weapon.

'Don't try it, Sheriff,' he warned. 'I'd hate to have to kill you. I reckon you can tell me a great deal about the troubles in Peso County.'

Baldy arrived, gun in hand, and stood to one side, covering the lawman. Grant looked from one to the other and then shrugged fatalistically.

'So you got back before I could leave,' he said.

'What do you hope to get from me?'

'Disarm him, Baldy. We'll talk to him back at the jail.'

Baldy grinned and went forward eagerly. He removed Grant's holstered six-gun, then checked the lawman for hidden weapons and found a small hide-out gun in a pocket. He shook his head as he showed it to the watching Belmont.

'Kinda sneaky, huh?' he said. 'Shows you what Herb is really like. And he ain't never been no great shakes as a sheriff. So get moving, Herb. You know where the jail is. Get along there without trouble and then you can tell us what's been going on around here.'

Grant walked to the door, his expression bleak. When he reached the street he paused and looked around as if hoping for assistance from some unexpected quarter. Belmont was alert to his surroundings as they started along the street towards the jail, and they all halted when a voice called to them. Turning quickly, Belmont saw Roscoe Dayne approaching. The deputy was grinning. His right arm was in a sling and his left hand was resting on the butt of a holstered six-gun.

'I'm on my way to take over the jail,' Dayne said. 'And it kinda looks like you got the sheriff under arrest. Is that a fact?'

'It sure is.' Baldy waggled his sixshooter. 'And I got a wish that Herb will try and make a break for it. That'd make my day and rid the county of a real snake.'

'It's about time your wrongdoin' got an airing, Sheriff,' Dayne said. 'You've been playing a helluva game.'

'If you got any proof of Grant's wrongdoing then

make a statement at the office,' Belmont said, easing his gun into its holster as they continued.

They walked along the sidewalk until they heard rapidly approaching hooves sounding at their backs. Belmont turned instantly, hand dropping to the butt of his gun. A rider was coming fast along the street pursued by four riders. Belmont drew his gun immediately. The foremost rider was Sam Bartleman, the Cattleman's Association detective.

Bartleman pulled his horse to a slithering halt beside them and dust flew as he sprang from his saddle. He grinned tensely at Belmont, his face flushed and perspiring.

'You wanted to get your hands on some of the rustlers, Clay,' he said breathlessly. 'Well, these four coming up are cow thieves in the flesh, and you'll have to help me take them. One of them is Cal Snark and another is Crow, the half-breed.'

The four riders hauled on their reins and halted a dozen yards away. For a moment they sat motionless, and Belmont spoke swiftly to Dayne.

'Take Grant to the jail and lock him in, Roscoe,' he said. 'Don't let him get away from you.'

'He'll be in a cell whenever you want him,' the deputy replied.

Belmont returned his attention to the four riders.

'This is the law,' he called. 'Get down from your horses and put up your hands. You're under arrest.'

His harshly spoken words galvanized the four men into frenzied action and they reached for their guns, intent on fighting. Belmont threw down on Snark, who was on the left, and blasted him out of the saddle with a shot that hurled thunderous echoes across the silent town. Baldy took on Crow, on the right, and knocked him over backwards with a .45

slug. One of the man's feet snagged in a stirrup and he was dragged away along the street as his horse fled. Bartleman fired and his bullet took the third rustler through the centre of the forehead, the deadly impact sending a gory splash of blood and shattered brain over the fourth man.

The remaining rustler ducked away, trying to turn his horse, but the animal cavorted and he lost his gun as he almost pitched out of his saddle. He straightened, found three steady guns covering him, and quickly raised his hands.

'Get down and keep your hands high,' Belmont called, and the man hastily vacated his saddle.

'These four chased me in from Orton's line shack,' Bartleman said dourly. 'I got a mite too close to their camp and was spotted. But I got the dead-wood on them, Clay. There's one big rustling gang working under a man named Charles Orton. Yeah, I said Orton. He's Kane Orton's brother, and he's responsible for all the rustling in Peso County. He made a mistake yesterday by lifting the Bar C herd, and the Bar C outfit caught up with them and they shot it out. The rustlers took off but returned, catching Bar C on the hop. Bar C was chased back to their ranch, and I don't know what happened there. But I was spotted then and had to light out fast. It's lucky for me you were on the street.'

'So, now we're getting down to it,' Belmont said. 'Kane Orton's got a brother who's a rustler. That point answers a lot of the questions goin' round in my mind. Some of the hardcases I've met have mentioned the name Orton, and I thought they meant the KO rancher himself. Now I know different. What are your plans, Sam? We're cleaning up around here. Do you wanta pitch in and help? I can promise you plenty of action.'

'I'll stick around,' Bartleman said. 'There are too many rustlers for me to handle out there on the range. When I lit out fast Charles Orton was on his way to see his brother, and there was gonna be some kind of a showdown. But I got a feeling the crooked bunch, what's left of 'em, is on the way to town. I reckon there's a big showdown coming.'

'There was a bunch of them expected at dawn out at Bar C,' Baldy said. 'And if they showed up there as expected I figure there won't be many of them left by the time Bar C and Flying W get through with them.'

Taking the surviving rustler with them, they continued to the law office, where Dayne was in the act of locking Herb Grant in a cell. The deputy grinned when he turned to Belmont.

'Nice shooting out there,' he remarked. 'And I figure you've got Herb worried. He just offered me five hundred bucks to turn him loose.'

'He ain't going anywhere,' Belmont said. 'Baldy, watch the street. That shooting will attract every badman in town.'

'You're right.' The ex-Ranger peered through one of the windows overlooking the street. 'Yeah. There's a bunch of men coming now. I can see Sim Goymer and Fred Stoll with Muley Hogben, and Hackett and Brewer are with them. Those two are the men who tried to kidnap Tilda at the livery barn when you put a stop to them.' Baldy massaged the top of his head. 'I got laid low then and it still hurts. Mebbe I can repay that blow with interest, huh? It looks like we got a fight on our hands, Clay. That bunch is loaded for bear. Heck, we better check our shooting irons.'

Belmont went to the window and peered out, his

lips pulling into a thin, uncompromising line when he saw the approaching men. Goymer, the town marshal, had his right arm in a sling and was carrying a shotgun with the butt tucked under his left armpit. All the other men were heavily armed, some carrying rifles in addition to their holstered six-guns.

'They're loaded for bear all right,' Belmont observed. 'We better get out on the street and face 'em down. They may not want to fight in the open.'

'Whatever you say.' Bartleman's eyes were gleaming. 'I know for a fact that Hogben is a rustler. I'd like to take him, Clay. He gave me some stick out at KO when I first went there.'

'He's yours,' Belmont replied, opening the street door.

He led the way outside, crossing the sidewalk to step down into the dust of the street, and his gaze did not waver from the five men advancing along the street side by side, spread out with space between them to minimize their target area. They had the finality about them of men committed to action with no alternative.

Hogben uttered a shout when he saw Belmont, and began to pull his six-gun, but stayed the movement when Baldy, Bartleman and then Roscoe Dayne appeared and spread out across the street. Sim Goymer did not hesitate in his approach. He came along steadily, tall and thin, his left hand clutching the shotgun, and Belmont noted that the man was wearing a holstered six-gun on his left side and had a choice of weapons.

'That's close enough,' Belmont called. 'You five men are wanted by the law so drop your weapons and raise your hands. We got you where the hair's short!'

Hogben uttered a yell and unlimbered his gun, his

action setting them all into motion. Sim swung up the long barrel of the shotgun, stepping back half a pace as he did so to balance himself. The others also reached for their guns. Belmont drew smoothly, and very fast. He snapped a shot at Goymer, beating all other action by a long, interminable moment.

Goymer took the bullet in the chest. Belmont saw blood fly at the impact. The tall marshal went backwards another half step, then resumed his interrupted action as if he had not been hit. The twin muzzles of the shotgun began to lift again, and Belmont fired a second time, canting his muzzle slightly, and a torrent of blood burst out of Goymer's forehead and cascaded down his thin face. He spun away and dropped inertly into the thick dust, legs kicking and body jerking spasmodically as he died. Gunsmoke flared and began to drift on the morning breeze.

Gunfire raged for endless moments. Bartleman put two slugs into Muley Hogben and got no reaction from the big man, although blood showed on the rustler's broad chest. Hogben returned fire, and Bartleman felt the smash of a bullet in his left shoulder. He started to fall, but braced his legs, making an effort to maintain fire at Hogben.

Baldy operated with the speed and precision of long practice and tough experience. He beat Fred Stoll to the draw and thumbed off a single shot that hit the deputy town marshal dead centre. Stoll stiffened under the impact, released his gun, which thudded into the dust, and then went down inertly, like a tree falling in a storm.

Roscoe Dayne had a fixed smile on his fleshy face. He was not accustomed to using a gun left-handed and felt awkward as he drew the weapon. Hackett and Brewer were directly opposite him and he took them on. His first shot hit Hackett about waist level and the rustler spun around before attempting to hobble away towards the nearest cover. Brewer fired then, and Dayne thought he had been kicked in the chest by a mule. He fired at Brewer as he unhinged at the waist like a rusty door, and pain flared through his body. Brewer went down heavily and lay still. Dayne was dimly aware of the dust of the street rushing up towards his face, and was faintly surprised because he had no sensation of falling. Then a black curtain dropped abruptly before his eyes and his limbs jerked convulsively as he died.

Bartleman dropped to one knee, trying to favour his left shoulder. Pain was flaring through him with all the heat of a forest fire. He could not believe what was happening. He had put three bullets into big Muley Hogben and the man was still standing and working his pistol. Bartleman sensed that this was one fight he could well lose, and desperation spurted through him. He shifted his aim slightly and triggered two more shots. The first slug took Hogben cleanly in the left eye and blasted on through the brain, and the second bullet smacked into Hogben's heart, boring through ribs and flesh before bursting that vital organ asunder. Hogben died on his feet and fell heavily into the dust, spilling blood from his wounds.

The urgent sounds of shooting cut off suddenly, and echoes began to growl away into the distance. Belmont had emptied his gun and now he saw that Hackett had reached an alley mouth to prop himself up against a corner and begin to lift his gun into action. Belmont reached desperately for fresh shells, but a shot blasted out from across the street and a bullet bored through Hackett's chest, pitching him over sideways and dropping him lifelessly into the dust.

Belmont looked around quickly as he stuffed fresh shells into his smoking weapon, wondering who had bought into the fight and saved his life. He sighed heavily when he saw Jake McGruder standing on the opposite sidewalk, a smoking six-gun in his hand and a big grin on his face. Belmont nodded and waved an acknowledging hand, then turned to survey the grim scene through narrowed eyes. Gunsmoke was thick around the street and he could feel it clogging his nostrils, sickly and acrid. He saw that all the badmen were down in the dust, and so were Dayne and Bartleman. Baldy was in the act of bending over Bartleman. Belmont went across to where the range detective lay, fearing the worst and hoping against hope that he was wrong.

'I'll be all right,' Bartleman was saying in answer to Baldy's inevitable question. 'I've had worse than this.'

Belmont turned and bent over Roscoe Dayne, and his heart seemed to miss a beat when he saw that the deputy was dead. He straightened, recalling his misgivings about the man when he first walked into the law office. But Dayne had played it straight all the way.

'Clay, take a look.' Baldy's voice was laced with tension, and Belmont straightened and spun around, expecting more trouble. His gun lifted to cover two horses coming at a walk towards them along the street, but he stayed his action when he recognized Kane Orton, who was leading the second horse which bore a man face down across the saddle. The KO rancher looked as if he had been in a fight.

His face was bruised and streaked with blood.

Orton reined up before Belmont and slid wearily from his saddle. He looked around at the sprawled bodies in the street and shook his head in disbelief, his narrowed eyes overbright with shock.

'I was hoping to get here before this started,' he said tiredly. 'But it's been quite a night.' He jerked a thumb at the inert figure roped to the saddle of the second horse. 'This is my brother. Charles. You should know that he's back of the rustling and everything else bad that's been happening in the county. He's bossed a gang of rustlers for years, and decided to look me up a few months ago. The trouble was, he brought his gang along with him, and they've been giving me hell ever since. Charles put Hogben in on my spread to keep me under his control.'

Belmont moistened his dry lips. He noted Doc Judd hurrying along the sidewalk towards them, medical bag in hand. 'I was out at Bar C last night,' he said, 'and helped stop a big attack made by the rustlers. I heard the name Orton mentioned a few times and figured it was you they were talking about.'

'What I told you last night about Bar C stealing my herd was wrong,' Orton shrugged, his face stiff. 'That's what I was told by my brother. He wanted me to join in the rustling with him, and when I wouldn't he set it up to look as if Bar C was guilty, and I fell for it. But, Charles got desperate after attacking the Bar C ranch and insisted that I join him and use my outfit to smash Bar C. When I refused, Charles came after me. He tried to kill me. Me! His own brother. He must have gone loco. When he pulled a gun on me I shot him like I would a mad dog. He'd gone too far, and had to be stopped. It fell to me to pull the trigger on him and I put an end to him.'

Hooves sounded along the street and alarm surged through Belmont. He glanced over his shoulder and saw a score of riders coming fast towards them.

'Get to cover, Baldy,' he called. 'This could be the last of them coming in.'

'Nope. ' Baldy grinned. 'That ain't what I'm seeing. Them's Bar C and Flying W riders, and there's a buggy behind them with Tilda and Asa in it.'

Belmont ejected spent shells from his gun and thumbed fresh loads into the cylinder. The riders came up and surged around them in a loose circle, and a dozen men began to speak at once. Baldy was waving his arms and talking at the top of his voice.

The buggy arrived and Belmont walked to it. Tilda was smiling, and Asa, his wounded leg bandaged and propped up on the seat, held out his hand for Belmont to shake.

'They came at us again well before dawn,' he said, 'and had the hell shot out of them. I'll bet there ain't a single rustler left in the whole county now. We got some prisoners, and the most interesting fact we learned from one of them is that Herb Grant, the sheriff, was in on the crookedness.'

'Not any more,' Belmont replied, relaxing for the first time since riding into the county. 'We jailed Grant this morning and it will be interesting to hear what he's got to say.'

Relief was large inside Belmont. The shooting was over, but there was a whole lot of talking to be done before the business would be laid bare. But the leaders were down and the details would take care of themselves.

He looked around the street. Townsfolk were

emerging from cover now the shooting was over, and he realized that he knew very few of them, even though he had put his life on the line for them. But that was how it always was, and he didn't for a minute think that anything would change.

He would spend a quiet day taking statements to get a clear picture of what had happened, and then would come orders to ride on to another community, where the whole grim business would recur.